Wolf!

Geoffrey Malone spent most of his childhood in Africa and avoided any formal education until the age of eleven. After school in England, he spent sixteen years as a soldier, then joined a Canadian public relations firm in Toronto. During all this time, he travelled widely and developed a fascination with animals in the wild. He returned to Britain in 1991, determined to become a children's author.

He has written six books for children, each one with a powerful and closely-observed animal interest. His story of a fox, *Torn Ear*, won the 2001 French Children's Book of the Year Award and the Prix Enfants grands-parents Européen. In England, *Elephant Ben* was shortlisted for the 2001 Stockton Children's Book of the Year Award.

Wolf! draws on his knowledge of life in remote North American communities and the age-old clash between humans and animals at the far edges of civilisation.

Wolf!

GEOFFREY MALONE

**Hodder
Children's
Books**

a division of Hodder Headline Limited

A Catalogue record for this book is available
from the British Library

ISBN 0 340 85065 5

Typeset by Avon Dataset Ltd, Bidford-on-Avon, Warks

Printed and bound in Great Britain by
Clays Ltd, St Ives plc

Hodder Children's Books
A division of Hodder Headline Limited
338 Euston Road
London NW1 3BH

To Marcus and Fergus

One

Marak raced ahead of the pack. A long grey shadow bounding silently through the endless forest. A starving wolf with hollow sides in a desperate pursuit of food.

Claw, his mate, had heard the moose coming half an hour ago when it had still been starlight. Even for a wolf, her hearing was acute. The herd had been five kilometres away when she had frozen in mid-stride, barking for silence.

Sixty seconds later, they could all hear it. The unmistakable sound of antlers clacking against branches and the soft thud of hooves plunging through the snow. But by then, the pack was racing light-footed after Marak, the leader, their stomachs churning with hunger and anticipation. None of them had eaten in the past four days and nights. And after the long, bitter winter, they were all dangerously weak.

It had been the worst winter Marak and Claw could ever remember. Food had been scarce almost since the first snows in November. By January, there were no caribou or forest deer to be found. The pack was reduced to hunting rodents and even birds.

Then in February, new blizzards had come roaring in from the north and dumped two metres more snow over the land. In despair, the pack huddled together in the old den where they had all been born. Three had died then, their bodies rigid as iron in the killing frosts. Finally, ten nights ago, Marak had led the pack out of their old territory and headed south into the unknown.

Now Marak barked a sharp order and they halted. He looked back and waited for Claw to join him. The rest of the pack watched. Two of the yearlings slumped full-length on the ground; their long red tongues licking at the snow. Marak bared his teeth and snarled at them. There was meat nearby. Life for all of them. They must make this one, last effort.

Claw was quivering with excitement. She stood beside him, her nose touching his, silently reassuring

2

him. The pack would make a kill. She rubbed her head against his neck and her certainty gave Marak new strength.

His fur bristled. He spun round to face the pack, challenging them to disobey. Not one of them dared meet his eye. Then he was away, scrambling up through the underbrush, his tail streaming out behind him. The hunt was on!

They chased after him, leaping over fallen trees, skirting boulders, scrambling up the steep hillsides. Their eyes never leaving the leader. Terrified of falling behind to face a solitary death. Marak listened to their laboured breathing and knew just how weak they had all become. He squeezed between two thick bushes, then stood motionless, hardly daring to move.

In the valley below, the herd of moose pushed through the trees in a clumsy, jostling flood. Their breath rose in a steamy mist that settled on the wolf's tongue, filling his mouth with saliva and longing. He whimpered in hunger.

Claw looked at him, her eyes bright with triumph. She licked his face urging him on. Behind them, he could hear the rest of the pack fretting with impatience. Only their instinctive discipline stopped them from racing down on the herd.

Marak barked an order. In single file the pack trotted along the crest line, staring down at the herd, searching for a possible victim. The moose soon spotted them and broke into a ponderous gallop. The bulls bellowed defiance, tossing their huge antlers while the cows bunched closer together.

The wolves followed at a fast lope for the next kilometre, driving themselves to keep up with the herd. And all the time their sharp eyes studied the moose, picking out individual animals and watching for any sign of weakness, age, disease or lameness. Another kilometre went by and still the herd lumbered on.

There was a tightness in Marak's chest, and a sudden floating sensation behind his eyes. He shook his head angrily. He looked over his shoulder and saw the gap opening up between Claw and the rest of the pack. He knew what it meant. Without meat, they would all die sometime over the next two days. But if they now used up what little strength they had left following the herd, they would drop in their tracks and never get up. And then Marak saw the old bull with the stiff front leg.

The bull was massive. He stood two metres high

at the shoulder and must have weighed over four hundred kilograms. His antlers were fully spread and heavy. His chest and shoulders were scarred with wounds from ruts long ago. He ran clumsily, his flanks heaving, doing his best to keep up.

The wolves kept pace with him, studying the way the bull was trying to keep the weight off his arthritic knee. Certainty grew in Marak's mind. This was their prey! Claw sensed it too and barked encouragement. As one, the pack turned and came racing down the side of the hill, their feet kicking up puffs of snow. Then they were running alongside the old moose.

The herd panicked and bunched even closer, tossing their heads and bellowing. The old bull was carried along with the stream. Marak watched the froth drip from his mouth. The bull stared across at him. Marak met his glance and held it. The bull looked away quickly, his eyes rolling with fear. Marak's blood surged and he barked loudly. The others understood and took up the chorus of triumph.

Slowly, inexorably, the bull began to fall behind. He began to roll from side to side, in exhaustion. Then he stumbled, dropping heavily on to his weak knee, forcing the rest of the herd to flow round him.

The bull swung his head and saw a dense stand of saplings only thirty metres away. He blundered towards it, snorting with pain. The rest of the herd galloped past, happy to leave him as the sacrifice for their own survival. The great moose forced his way through thick, springy bushes into the middle of the thicket. Then he turned and faced the pack, shaking with fear.

The wolves came after him, howling with frustration. For a while they milled around, uncertain what to do next. The bull watched and bellowed at them. Impulsively, Claw ran straight towards him, following the path he had made. Her shoulders hunched and her belly brushing the ground. A huge hoof smashed down, missing her head by a couple of centimetres. The bull lashed out again. Shaken, she scrambled back towards the others. A frontal attack was hopeless.

For an hour, the wolves squirmed through the undergrowth trying to find the best way to attack. But the brushwood was dense. It seemed to have a life of its own. It caught at their coats and pulled them back. And the pack realized that whichever way they attacked, the moose would have enough time to crush their skulls or break their spines, with a single, well-placed kick. They flopped down in front of the moose and stared at him with hate-filled eyes.

Time passed. The sun began to climb up the sky. It grew warmer. The bull tossed his antlers and a lump of snow fell wetly on his head. He snorted and stamped his feet. He was growing bored and impatient to rejoin the herd.

Marak sensed his mood and an idea came to him. He looked across at Claw. Silently, they communicated. Very slowly, Marak got to his feet, stretching elaborately and yawning. His jaws opened in a long, tired grin. Then without looking back, he walked round the side of the thicket and trotted away.

The moose swung his head to watch. Without thinking, he took a couple of small steps forward to get a better view. Then he remembered the rest of the pack and jumped back into cover. As he did so his antlers snagged in the branches of a tree. Panic-stricken, he wrenched them clear.

But he needn't have worried. Not one of the wolves had moved. The bull snorted and pawed the ground. Five minutes later, Claw walked away. The others followed one by one until only the youngest wolf was left on guard. Soon, she rolled over on her side and fell asleep.

A long silence fell. The moose stirred uneasily, occasionally rolling his eyes. He knew the wolves were still in the vicinity but no matter how hard he listened, there was no sound of them. The open space in front of him grew wider and wider and more inviting. It beckoned to him. The rest of the herd would have stopped running as soon as the wolves had disappeared. The old bull knew they'd be grazing now, kicking away the snow to get at the grass that lay underneath. Back in the herd he'd be safe again.

And then the last remaining wolf sat up, shook herself and headed for the far side of the valley. She slipped into the trees and disappeared. Slowly, bravely, his whole body trembling, the moose edged forward. With a sudden bold step he came out of the thicket. He looked carefully around him, drew a deep breath and ran!

Two

The rifle was new and shiny. It smelled of gun oil and cold steel. The man's fingers caressed the long blue barrel. Lovingly he laid his cheek against the polished wood of the stock and sighed with pleasure. He had ordered it from a gun shop a month ago. It had come up yesterday with the weekly parcel delivery from Laramie, the State capital, two hundred miles to the south. It had cost over a thousand dollars.

He turned towards the window and closed one eye. The cross hairs inside the sniper sight stood out black and sharp against the snow-covered airfield outside. He shook his head admiringly, 'Worth every cent!' He turned and looked at the other man. 'Hope you know where to look, Mr Daniels,' he said. 'Only,

I've hunted them before and they ain't easy to spot from the air.'

The other man said nothing. Instead, he bent down and began to pull on a pair of fur-lined flying boots. He was older and grizzled. A big man with a weather-beaten face. A man used to giving orders. He stood up and stamped his feet, then walked over to the map that covered most of one wall.

'Right here!' he said, tapping the map with a calloused finger. 'They're in the hills, other side of the river. We heard 'em howling last night. First time we've had wolves here in ten years!' He glared at the hunter. 'I've got ten thousand cattle out there. Most of them'll be calving in a week's time.'

He paused. 'I'll find them. You just make damn certain you shoot straight, Tom Shaw. That's what I'm paying for!'

He turned away and put on a heavy leather jacket. The coffee machine in the corner of the little room gurgled. Tom Shaw bent and picked up a battered holdall. 'Ammunition,' he explained. 'Got enough in here to start World War Three!'

They stepped outside into the biting cold of the dawn. The wind slammed the door shut behind them. The mucus in their noses immediately began to freeze. A woman in the tiny control tower gave them a friendly wave as they went past. Daniels raised his hand in acknowledgement.

All round, the snow glittered in the early March sunshine. Spring was coming. Soon the icicles would start to melt and the cycle of life would begin all over again. But that was still some weeks away. Ahead of them, the helicopter was a splash of brilliant red.

Daniels walked round it, untying the blades. He was very proud of the helicopter. He had bought it three years ago when beef prices were high. He was the biggest rancher in the county and it seemed only right that he should own such a machine.

They clambered inside and strapped themselves in. It was very cramped. Tom Shaw rummaged in his bag, opened a cardboard box and placed it between his feet. Fifty long-nosed, steel-tipped bullets gleamed dully in the lights of the instrument panel. Then he put on the headphones. Daniels was talking to the tower.

The rancher turned a key and the engine coughed once, then roared, belching oily smoke. Above them, the blades started to swing. Seconds later they were in the middle of a blizzard of snow and noise. 'Good luck!' they heard the woman in the tower call over

11

the headphones. 'Bring a couple back for me. I sure could do with a new winter coat!'

Daniels eased the control column back and moments later the helicopter rose into the clear, frozen sky. It circled twice then, with its nose tilting steeply downwards, roared towards the distant line of trees.

Three

Adrenalin surged through the moose's veins. He felt no pain in his knee, only a heady sense of triumph. The sun was warm on his face. The air smelt of wood resin and he knew the sap was starting to rise. He broke into a heavy canter.

High above, Marak watched and kept pace with him. He saw the birch trees shaking as the bull crashed past. He could hear every laboured breath the old moose took and the harsh, rasping sound it made deep in his lungs. Marak squinted into the sun, searching for Claw and the others. They were somewhere in front, waiting to spring the trap. He put his head back and called.

The moose heard Claw's answering howl and shuddered. The wolves had tricked him! They had

13

not gone away. They were all round him. The huge muscles in his back legs bunched and he jumped high over a fallen tree that blocked his path. Marak howled briefly and ran, sure-footed, to cut off the old bull.

The moose heard him and knew Marak was closing in. Confused, he slewed round and burst through a straggly line of alders. It was a mistake, and the old bull knew it. Large rocks reared up through the snow in front of him. Stunted trees bristled in large clumps, too high to jump but not thick enough to hide in. There was no clear way through.

He slipped. Pain shot through his knee. Then a flicker of movement caught his eye. A hundred metres away four wolves were bounding towards him. His legs shook. He couldn't move. He stood there, swaying from side to side, moaning in disbelief. The wolves were spreading out, coming at him from both sides. Somehow he was running again. Awkwardly. Tossing his antlers in distress. And Claw knew he was quite lame.

She watched him stumble, then recover and hobble on. She saw the lightly-built yearlings snapping at his legs and leaping for his head.

Confused, the old bull reared up, lashing out with his front hooves.

Claw gathered what strength she had left and attacked from the rear. The yearlings saw her and set up a fresh chorus of howls. Distracted, the old moose shied away, then bellowed in terror as she leapt high across his back.

The moose bucked and leapt sideways. Claw hung on grimly, the taste of hot blood making her giddy. She saw Marak racing beside them. The bull's antlers swung down, catching the wolf a glancing blow that sent him tumbling over the frozen ground. But Marak was already back on his feet and coming in again.

The moose's heart was bursting. A red film fogged his eyes. Out of it, a snarling face erupted into his own. Razor-sharp teeth ripped at his nose. The pain was intense. His eyes streamed with tears. He stumbled, careered headlong down a steep bank and skidded out on to an ice-covered lake.

His great feet splayed under him. He fell with a terrible crash, his body spinning uncontrollably for twenty metres across the ice. He tried to get up but his legs refused to obey him. The air was full of snarling and the smell of wolves. There was blood everywhere. All over his legs and pouring out of the hole in his neck. He collapsed, his body convulsing while the wolves climbed over him. Slowly, the light began to fade from his eyes.

Four

The bright yellow school bus came round the corner and drove carefully towards the waiting group of children. Ed Viccary sighed and hunched his shoulders down into the warmth of his anorak.

He was a stocky thirteen-year-old, with curly black hair and serious grey eyes. Gloomily he watched the bus approach, slush spraying from its wheels. In a few moments he would have to climb up inside and face the jeers and stupidity of Pete Daniels and his gang.

Beside him, Jessica, his younger sister was chatting animatedly with two friends. It was all right for her, Ed thought. She never had any problems making friends. She was only ten, but already had a well-developed, happy-go-lucky nature that most people liked. True, she had cried bitterly when they left New York six months ago, but within a week she had settled happily into this new school, eighteen hundred miles away in Wyoming.

Now she turned to him. 'What was the animal you and Jimmy were tracking in the woods last Saturday?' When he didn't answer, she tugged at his arm. He looked into her bright eyes and for a moment envied her happiness.

'Bobcat,' he told them. 'A big male,' he added shyly, looking round at their faces. 'He was marking out his territory. They mate at this time of year,' he added in explanation. One of the girls giggled. 'Ed knows just about every animal round here,' Jessica told them proudly.

Ed shook his head. 'Jimmy does. Not me,' he began to say, then the bus pulled up beside them, its doors flapping open. Faces peered down through steamed-up windows. 'C'mon guys! Hurry it up!' called the driver. She wore an Elliott Lake High School sweatshirt and blue tracksuit bottoms. 'We're a bit late this morning. Found a puncture when I got to the garage,' she explained with a bright smile.

Ed took a deep breath and climbed on board.

There was only one school in the area and the bus was already half full of children from the outlying farms. His heart sank as he surveyed the older boys at the back of the bus. They were all there, nudging one another and looking at him.

'I hate this place,' he thought and was immediately contrite, remembering his friend, little Jimmy Skagawa. Jimmy was a Native American and not much bigger than Jessica. He was a shy boy and a loner, like Ed. The two of them had quickly become good friends.

Besides, there was nothing really wrong with the little town of Elliott Lake or its surrounding hills and lakes, which teemed with wildlife. The people were friendly and had easily accepted the Viccarys as new neighbours. His parents were both vets and worked for old Mr Price, who had the largest surgery in town.

It was just this one individual who was ruining everything. Pete Daniels was a heavy, aggressive boy. He was a year older than Ed and had taken an instant and violent dislike to him. To make matters worse, his father was the biggest rancher for miles and the surgery's most important customer.

Jessica was prodding him in the back. 'Keep

moving!' she ordered. 'There's lots more people behind.' He set his face in a mask and walked as nonchalantly as he could along the gangway towards Pete Daniels and his friends. 'My Dad's taking us all on a Caribbean cruise next vacation,' Pete was saying in a loud voice. 'It's gonna cost more than twenty thousand dollars.'

Ed sat down beside a window and began wiping off the condensation with his sleeve. Pete raised his voice. 'My mom says it's only for classy folks.'

'So, no vets, eh?' someone laughed.

'Don't mention vets to my dad,' called a third. 'He got a bill, Friday. Wow! Was he mad! Said they charged way too much.'

Ed looked out of the window as the bus drove slowly down a road bordered by neat wood-frame houses.

'Yeah! That's what I hear,' agreed Pete, raising his voice still more. 'A rip-off. Been getting worse these past six months, ever since old man Price hired in some fancy help from back East.' They all laughed and waited.

Ed could see his mother standing beside her battered old Ford with its New York number plates. She was waving energetically. He wished she wouldn't. 'Look! It's Mom!' Jessica cried from the seat in front and waved back. Sheepishly, Ed waggled the fingers of one hand. Behind him, Pete and the others dissolved into laughter.

'Oh, my little baby!' he heard someone mock.

'Cool car!' another jeered.

Ed flushed as the anger rose inside him. Over supper last night, the Viccarys had discussed whether or not they could afford to replace the old pick-up. In the end, they had decided they couldn't. It would have to last another year.

'Hey, city boy!' Pete drawled. 'Where you going for Easter vacation?'

Jessica turned round in her seat. 'My dad's been asked to give a seminar on grizzly bears. Seventy environmentalists are coming from all over the world to hear him!' she told the bus proudly. 'And Ed's helping put together the slide show.'

'Grizzly bears!' exclaimed Pete in genuine astonishment. 'You're kidding!'

Jessica shook her head. 'No!' she told him firmly. 'It's going to be up in the Yellowstone National Park.'

Pete shook his head in disbelief. 'Grizzly bears!' he exclaimed. 'What the heck does your old man know about grizzly bears!'

'Sure you don't mean goldfish?' another boy scoffed.

'My dad worked in the Yellowstone for his Ph.D.,' Ed told them gruffly, looking straight ahead.

'And he's written articles about them in magazines and things,' Jessica protested. 'He's an expert.'

'I bet he's never even seen one,' Pete shouted. 'Got many grizzlies in New York?'

They all laughed. Ed swung round in his seat and stared at Pete Daniels. 'My dad worked on the grizzly resettlement project for two years. He knows more about them than anyone round here ever will.'

'The only good grizzly is a dead grizzly!' someone else shouted. 'They took three of our calves last summer.'

Pete was staring at Ed in disbelief. 'Are you telling us that your old man was the guy who brought all those damn bears to live round here?'

Ed nodded. 'He helped, yeah.' The rest of the bus was silent now. Ed looked round at them and shrugged. 'The bears were here thousands of years before humans.'

Pete's face flamed. 'And your pa's got the nerve

to come here and work as a vet! This is cattle country, city boy! We don't want crazies like him!'

There was a murmur of agreement. Jessica's eyes widened. Ed shook his head. 'There's more than enough food for every animal in the local ecosystem,' he protested.

Pete laughed in contempt. 'You just wait till I tell my dad that. He's gonna love it!' He grinned round at the others. 'My dad will have him sacked. You just wait and see!' And he kicked the back of Ed's seat.

The next moment, Ed was on his feet. 'Butt out, Hayseed!' he shouted. 'People like you went out with dinosaurs!'

Pete flung himself out of his seat and pushed his face very close to Ed's. 'How do you feel about wolves then, Viccary? Know all about them, do you? Think they're cute, eh? Only we've got a pack of them on our land!' His breath smelt hot and angry.

Ed looked away. Pete grabbed him by the shoulder. 'Like to know what my dad's doing right now?' he hissed. 'He's up in his helicopter shooting them. That's what!'

Ed flung his hand off. Daniels pulled his fist back. 'Hey! Stop that! Viccary! Daniels! Sit down or you'll be on report,' the driver shouted.

The bus drove round the town square, past the brick courthouse with its tall flagpole and out towards the huddle of school buildings at the edge of town. It was not a good start to the day.

Five

The men in the helicopter were not having much luck. Tom Shaw yawned and rubbed his eyes. 'Seeing spots,' he confided over the headphones. 'Been staring at too many trees for too long.'

Daniels grunted and watched the helicopter's shadow race away in front of them. High overhead a pair of eagles soared. He leaned forward and tapped the fuel gauge. 'Half an hour left,' he told Shaw. 'Maybe a bit over. We'll make one more sweep, then head back to refuel.'

'And get some coffee,' Shaw said plaintively.

They flew on for another five minutes. The terrain was steeper here, the valleys narrower. Effortlessly, Daniels followed the twists and turns of the ground, keeping the machine twenty metres above the treetops. He loved flying and flew instinctively while he thought about other things.

So it took a few moments before his mind fully registered. 'Hey! Take a look at that,' he cried, pointing downwards. He shot an angry glance at Shaw. 'You asleep or something!'

Shaw sat up and began looking around.

'Tracks!' shouted Daniels. 'There's been a herd along here.' He banked the helicopter and stared down. 'Big herd!'

'You're right!' Shaw told him. 'Recent too. See how fresh those stains are? An hour ago? Not much more.'

'OK. So keep your eyes skinned!' cried Daniels impatiently. 'If there's any wolves about, you can bet your bottom dollar they'll be hanging round here!'

They flew on slowly, scanning the valley sides and bottom. 'There! Dead ahead!' Shaw exclaimed. 'Moose,' he confirmed a couple of seconds later.

Daniels took the helicopter higher, then hovered to one side to avoid panicking the herd. 'Well, they look happy enough,' he said grudgingly. He tapped the gauge again. 'Time to go.'

'Reckon you'll find this place again?' Shaw asked.

Daniels swung the helicopter through three

hundred and sixty degrees. 'Yep!' he exclaimed. 'See that old railroad bridge? Stands out a mile. That's our reference point.'

Then Shaw was grabbing at his wrist and shouting. The helicopter lurched sideways. 'What the hell!' Daniels swore, pulling back on the control bar. Shaw was leaning over him, his voice distorting in the headphones. 'Down there! Down on the ice!'

Marak flapped an ear. There was a wasp or something buzzing round. It just wouldn't go away. Lazily, he rubbed a paw over his head. He had eaten ten kilograms of meat and fallen almost immediately into a delicious sleep. For the first time in months he felt content.

The others lay stretched out beside the carcass, equally comatose. There was enough food to last them for another five days. Marak sighed and opened an eye. The buzzing was getting louder. Much louder. Too loud for a wasp. Much too loud! The hair on his face stiffened.

He sat up and looked around, fully alert. Claw was on her feet looking over his shoulder and snarling. Now the whole pack was staring at the strange-looking dragonfly.

There was a flash of brilliant light. A sharp crack. And Claw was tossed into the air, screaming. Marak spun towards her. Another bang and the yearling beside him collapsed. There was blood everywhere. Marak tried to run. His feet slipped just as the next bullet slammed him down full-length on to the ice. Then he was falling head over heels into spinning oblivion.

Six

Amy Viccary enjoyed driving. But she was still more at home on the twelve-lane New Jersey Turnpike than this country dirt road. She gripped the steering wheel tightly as the pick-up bumped and skidded its way back to Elliott Lake across the frozen ruts.

It had been a long day even before the emergency phone call had summoned her out to a farm, fifty miles away. A prize mare was in trouble foaling. Amy had got there just in time to turn the foal's head round for a normal birth. The farmer was delighted and insisted she stay to lunch.

Tired but content, she was singing along with the radio, happy to be going home. She would be there in half an hour. Rick and the children would be waiting for her. There was a stew all ready to go into the microwave. Then a much-needed early bed.

She flicked the headlights on. The frost sparkled back at her. It had sure been a bitter winter, she reflected. Colder even than New York – and that was saying something! She braked and swung the wheel to avoid a large pothole. The headlights jumped and for a second, she thought she saw a dark shadow moving at the edge of their beam. She straightened up and drove on slowly.

The shadow was still there. Keeping just ahead of the truck. She put her foot down on the accelerator and the headlights swept forward, tunnelling between the trees on either side. And then two yellow eyes were staring at her! And she was looking at the biggest wolf she had ever seen!

She gave a cry of terror and braked hard. She couldn't help it. This was a fear as old as history itself. A primitive folk memory that stretched back to the cavemen. The back wheels of the truck skidded and the vehicle slipped sideways. The engine raced and stalled. The radio went dead.

The wolf stared into the headlights, seeming to look straight at her, while Amy struggled to think rationally. She was perfectly safe in the cab. She had her mobile on the seat beside her. And she knew there was no record anywhere in America of a wolf ever attacking a human being.

She took several deep breaths to calm the pounding of her heart and watched the wolf turn away. There was a black stain on the snow where it had stood. It was limping, moving brokenly. Then the front legs gave way and the wolf slumped down on to its side.

She grabbed the door handle. Then hesitated, staring wide-eyed at the animal. The wolf's back leg scraped at the ground. Its head came up and swung towards the headlights. She willed it back on its feet. Time stood still while the entire world shrank into this tiny stage.

The wolf gave a shudder and collapsed. She picked up the mobile and dialled for help.

Seven

Marak heard the other vehicle approaching long before Amy saw the welcoming flash of its headlights. As he drifted in and out of consciousness, he heard the slam of doors and the sound of human voices. Heavy boots crunched towards him and he knew real fear for the first time in his life.

Panic-stricken, he tried to stand but his legs buckled under him. He felt no pain, only an overwhelming desire to sleep. His head swooped and roared as the fever burned deep inside him. He pitched forward and lay inert, panting loudly as the life force drained away.

He remembered Claw. She was calling him. He bounded across the snow towards her. There was a sharp stab in his back leg. He opened his eyes and looked up at the human. He could smell the sweat on the man's skin. Marak tried to snarl but his lips were numb. Claw was with him again, nuzzling and licking his nose. The pack was all round him. It was time to go hunting.

Eight

'He's been shot!' exclaimed Rick Viccary, squatting down beside the wolf.

'Rick! Don't get that close!' Amy warned. 'You've got to give the tranquillizer more time!'

Rick sat back on his haunches and shook his head. 'We've got to move fast. We'll be lucky to get him back alive. That's a real bad wound, Amy. He's lost a lot of blood.' Cautiously he slid his hand over the wolf's shoulder and gently nipped his ear. 'It's OK,' he told her. 'He's out cold.'

He stared down at Marak. 'He's big, isn't he? Must be almost two metres nose to tail. What the heck's he doing this far south? Hasn't been a wolf down here in years, I heard. Wonder what happened to the rest of the pack?' He rubbed the wolf's fur between his fingers. 'He's in pretty bad shape. Here! Feel how thin his coat is.'

'So let's get him home then,' Amy said impatiently. 'Fast!'

Rick nodded. He went over to his vehicle and returned with a large syringe. 'Antibiotics. The strongest we've got.'

They worked in nervy silence, strapping tight Marak's front and back legs. Then Rick took a deep breath and bent over the wolf's head. Slowly, he eased a reinforced leather muzzle up over Marak's jaws. 'Biggest one I could find,' he grunted. He buckled it fast with difficulty, wiped the sweat from his forehead and grinned at Amy. 'Glad that part's over.'

'We'll need a full-sized stretcher for him,' Amy considered. They placed it on the snow beside the wolf. Then slid their hands and arms under him. 'Ready and lift!' ordered Rick.

They rolled Marak on to the stretcher. It was surprisingly easy. 'He's so light!' Amy exclaimed a moment later. 'Can't weigh much more than a big dog. A labrador or something.'

'Not much more,' Rick agreed. The wolf's tail and back legs hung over the stretcher. 'He's just skin and bone. Let's get him inside.'

They lifted the stretcher round to the back of Rick's 4×4 and carefully slid it inside. Amy leaned over Marak and lifted an eyelid. 'He's right out.'

Rick locked the back doors. He began to grin. 'A wolf!' he chuckled. 'Never been this close to one!'

'We'd best operate as soon as we get back,' Amy told him. 'We can put him in that big cage afterwards. If he survives.'

Rick made a face. 'If he survives!'

'I'll call the surgery and warn them we'll have a full-grown timber wolf in the hospital,' Amy said. 'Just in case they get in tomorrow morning before we do!'

'And I'll tell the kids we're on our way back with a wolf!'

Much later that evening, they all sat round the kitchen table finishing supper. The room was warm and cosy. Amy's eyes were closing.

'Will the wolf be all right now, Dad?' Jessica asked.

Ed watched his parents, trying to read their thoughts.

Amy looked at Rick and smiled wearily. 'Well, we've spent two hours working on him. So he's got some sort of a chance, I guess.'

Rick nodded. 'He should be OK. He was lucky. The bullet passed clean through him. It made a mess of a lot of soft tissue but missed all the vital organs. He's had a massive blood transfusion. But there's no serious damage.'

'There's always the shock thing, though,' Amy warned. 'We'll just have to keep our fingers crossed for the next forty-eight hours or so.'

Ed slapped his hand down on the table, interrupting them. They stared at him in surprise. 'Pete Daniels!' he cried. 'Of course! His father must have shot him!' Then seeing their blank expressions, Ed explained. 'He told me this morning that his dad was up in a helicopter looking to kill wolves. There's been a pack howling out on their ranch. This must be one of them!'

His parents exchanged glances and frowned. 'You sure about this?' Rick questioned.

'That's what Daniels said,' Ed replied.

'Please can we see the wolf tomorrow?' Jessica pleaded.

'Tomorrow or the day after,' Rick told her. 'Let's mend him first. When he's fit, we'll all go and say hello to him.'

'How big is he?' she asked.

'I've told you. Big enough!' Amy said, getting up. 'Now come on, you two. Eat up. It's late. You've got school tomorrow.'

'You going to tell Mr Price?' Ed asked.

His father thought for a moment. Then shook his head. 'He's in Florida on vacation. He'll be back at the weekend. No point bothering him now. No one's going to harm the wolf.'

'Wanna bet?' Ed muttered. But neither of his parents heard him.

Six hours later, Marak opened an eye and the pain came rushing back. It tore through his body, ripping at the stitches deep inside him with steel-tipped claws, crushing his lungs until he whimpered like a cub. He lay quite still, too weak to move, helpless against the onslaught. His head spun and ached until oblivion returned in a breaking wave of darkness.

It was better the next time. He forced himself up into a sitting position and stared around. He had no idea where he was. No recollection of how he had got here. Or how long he had been like this. There was no sky or earth. No scent of trees. No space. No distance. Just strange smells and noises he did not recognize.

He decided he must be in a den or a cave of some sort. He understood that. He pushed his nose between the bars, trying to force them apart. And failed. He tried again several times in different places. And failed again. Trapped! And his mouth was so dry!

There was water in a shiny bowl at one end of the cage. It smelt of human and he snarled at it, remembering the human's face peering down at him. It had rows of very small teeth and its breath stank. Marak sniffed at the bowl suspiciously then greedily lapped it dry.

It was so hot in here. And so still. With a glaring light overhead that was painful to stare at. The place belonged to humans! There was no way out. And the pain was coming back. He sank down and lay with his nose against the bars. He licked them and then lay still, enjoying their coolness. He gripped one with his teeth and sensed it was a dead thing. But he marvelled at its strength and hardness.

The noise in his head was growing louder. He remembered the red helicopter and saw the bright flashes shooting at him. He tried to dodge but was unconscious before his head dropped on to his paws.

Nine

The entire school knew about the wolf by lunchtime the next day. Jessica's friends were wide-eyed with excitement. 'Wow! You got a real live wolf in the surgery? Scary. Can we come and see?'

Some of the older girls were not so sympathetic. 'What's that thing doing in there anyway?'

'He's been shot,' Jessica explained. 'And he's very weak and lost a lot of blood. My dad's operated on him.'

'Well,' they told her. 'We're not bringing our pets in until that thing goes!'

Amongst Ed's classmates, only his friend Jimmy Skagawa was pleased. 'That's fantastic, Ed!' he exclaimed, grinning all over his face. 'Your folks are great people! I'll tell my grandpa. He'll be delighted.'

But for the rest of them, there was a sullen hostility which grew stronger as the day wore on. At the end of school, Pete Daniels and his friends cornered Ed outside the boiler house. There were six of them. They formed a half circle, forcing him back against the brick wall.

Pete Daniels put his hands on his hips and shouted at him. 'Hey, city boy! Is this stuff I'm hearing true?'

Ed shrugged and forced himself to look as relaxed as possible. They were all jerks, he thought. But this guy Daniels was the biggest one of the lot. 'Search me, Daniels,' he said coolly. 'I don't know what people tell an idiot like you.'

Pete Daniels flushed. This New York kid was just too smart for his own good. He looked round at the others and saw they felt the same. He took a step closer. He was taller than Viccary by a head. 'People are saying that your folks found a sick wolf and they've got it in the surgery.'

Ed nodded. 'Yep. My mum found it on a back road out of town. Seems like some jerk shot it.'

'Right on!' Pete interrupted, looking round at his friends. He punched his fist in the air and they all cheered. 'That'll be one of the pack my pa was hunting!'

'That figures,' Ed said with contempt. 'He's a rotten shot and he just left it to die.'

'So what's wrong with that?' one of the others shouted.

'You dumb cluck!' Ed replied scathingly. 'An animal can't help behaving the way it does any more than you can.' And the scorn in his voice was unmistakable.

Pete's face darkened. His fists bunched. 'Who the heck are you to give us all this rubbish!' He turned to his friends. 'What does he know about wolves? First, it's how wonderful grizzlies are. Now it's wolves.' He pushed Ed away. 'You make me sick!'

Someone hurled a snowball. It exploded in Ed's face. He staggered back against the wall, clutching at his eyes, blinded by the blow. Then they were on him, pulling him down, pummelling him, stuffing snow into his mouth and ears and down inside his clothes.

He lashed out with his fists but there were too many of them. Someone, Pete probably, knelt on his chest and banged his head on the icy ground.

The school bell rang. Reluctantly they stopped. Slowly, Ed sat up. Pete stood over him, smiling in triumph. 'Get out of here, Viccary,' he sneered. 'Go back to the city. We don't want your kind round here.' And then they were gone.

Ed cleaned himself up in the washroom. One side of his face felt raw. Ice-cold water ran down his back into his underpants. He towelled himself as best he could and considered. There was no point complaining to his form teacher. The others would deny it or say it was just a friendly snowball fight. Besides, he thought, they'd be expecting him to make a fuss.

He studied his face in the mirror. It was red and puffy-looking. He touched it and winced. He had a horrible feeling there'd be a bruise by morning. What would he tell his parents? He didn't want to mention Pete Daniels. Nor what the fight had been about. They'd only worry. No! He'd best say he had slipped and fallen over.

He splashed more cold water over it and reflected that he was going to be up against Pete Daniels and his crew for a very long time to come. Right now, the boy held the whip hand over him. Just like Daniels' father did over his own parents.

He thought about his mum and dad and wondered if this sort of bullying happened when you were an adult? There wouldn't be the physical thing of course. No one would actually get you down on the ice. But they could make you lose your job so you'd have no money for your family. He sighed and began to comb his hair.

He saw his friend Jimmy in the mirror and swung round to greet him.

'Pete Daniels did that to you?' Jimmy demanded, pointing at his face.

Ed shrugged. 'Looks worse than it is. Don't worry about it. I'll get my own back on him, you'll see. Maybe I'll start doing judo or something.'

Jimmy scowled. 'He's a pig,' he said. 'I hate him!'

Ten

Later that evening, the telephone rang at home. Amy Viccary answered it. She listened intently, then smiled. 'They'd love to,' she said and nodded at Ed and his sister. 'We're on our way.'

She replaced the receiver and said happily, 'Your father says you can come and have a look at the wolf. But you've got to be quiet!'

The surgery was in a modern, single-storey building. Rick Viccary met them at the front door. 'Great!' he enthused. 'Come on in.' Lucy Smith, the practice nurse, gave them a tight little smile, then bent her head over some paperwork. 'She's not very happy about something,' Jessica thought.

The animal hospital was in the basement. A set of rubber-edged stairs led down to it. Rick put a finger to his lips and carefully opened the door. The overhead lights hummed gently. The walls gleamed white and the floor was covered with green, non-slip tiles. There was a strong smell of antiseptic in the air.

A rabbit sat up on its hind legs and watched them. Its nose twitched. A solitary dog wagged its tail and whined to be let out. There were other animals in there but Ed's eyes went immediately to the large steel cage along the far wall.

The animal inside dominated the room. It was huge. Much bigger than an alsatian. The hair on the back of Ed's neck tingled. His chest felt tight. He hardly dared breathe. His eyes were riveted on the cage. Slowly, reverentially almost, he tiptoed over and stood looking down at the wolf.

Behind him he heard Jessica whisper, 'He's so beautiful.' And he was, Ed thought. He was magnificent. He gazed down in awe at the wolf who lay sprawled full-length, like a carefully discarded fur coat. The wolf's eyes were closed. He seemed to be smiling at something.

'He's a metre and three-quarters from nose to tail,' Rick told them proudly. 'And pure black all over. Not a white or grey hair to be found.'

Ed knelt down beside the cage. He had never seen a wild animal as close as this before. There was something in the sheer size of the wolf that took his breath away. He was enormous. He thought of the animal's power compared to his own puny strength, and shivered. This was Nature at her best.

He shivered. 'How old is he?'

'About four years,' Amy told him. 'They're fully grown by three. See how big his head and chest are?'

'Take a look at those jaws,' Rick laughed. 'Massive, eh? Remember Little Red Riding Hood?'

'He's laughing,' Jessica said, pointing. Ed noticed she was keeping her distance from the cage.

'How fast can he run?' he wanted to know.

'Anything up to thirty-five miles an hour top speed,' said his father.

'But they normally go at a fast trot,' Amy told them. 'Seven, eight miles an hour. They can keep it up for days. That's how they wear other animals down.'

'Once they've marked their prey, they just don't give up. They'll follow it for a week if necessary,' Rick added.

'Where did the bullet go?' demanded Jessica.

Rick told her. 'Straight through the lower

abdomen. In and out the other side. It didn't touch his lungs or liver or anything, though it was a pretty close thing. He was really lucky!'

'But he would still have died from the infection,' Amy added. 'That bullet took a whole lot of fur and debris in with it.'

'What's going to happen to him now?' Ed asked.

His parents smiled at one another. 'Well,' began his father. 'If he makes a full recovery, we'll contact the folks we know who run the wolf recolonization programme in the Yellowstone National Park.'

'Hey! That's a great idea!' exclaimed Ed.

'Why? What is it?' Jessica asked impatiently.

Ed turned to her, 'Ever wondered why there are no wolves in this state?'

'Or most others?' Amy agreed.

Jessica made a face. 'Because people have driven them out. Killed them all, I guess.'

'Especially the ranchers. Right, Dad?' Ed demanded.

Rick shrugged. 'Anyway,' he told her, 'that's all set to change. The government wants to bring 'em back into wilderness areas like the national parks. It's a big environmental project and you need wolves to maintain the ecology. They're top of the food chain. They're key players.'

'Sounds good to you guys?' Amy looked at her watch. 'I think it's time to go!'

That night, Rick Viccary opened a bottle of wine. 'Something truly wonderful has happened. Something we should all celebrate.' He smiled round at them and raised his glass. 'I'm just so glad we can all share in it as a family. Here's to the wolf! May he have many long years!'

'To the wolf!' they echoed. 'To the wolf!' Jessica nudged Ed. 'Won't that old Pete Daniels be mad when he finds out?'

Eleven

Rick was in the surgery examining a cat. The cat's owner was elderly and made crooning noises over it. The animal was in obvious pain and frightened. 'Just hold her still,' Rick warned, and gently ran the tips of his fingers over the animal's stomach.

'She's not as young as she used to be,' the old lady told him. 'Getting on a bit, like me. What do you think it is, doc?'

Rick frowned. 'Could be kidney trouble. I'd like you to leave her with me for the time being. I'll do some tests. Will that be OK?' The woman nodded.

Lucy Smith put her head round the door. 'There's someone to see you, Rick.'

There was an edge to her voice that made him look up. The cat squirmed round and scratched him viciously across the back of the hand. 'Lucy!' he snapped, sucking at the blood, 'can't you see I'm busy with a patient?'

Lucy looked uncomfortable. She hesitated, then came further into the room. 'I'm sorry, Rick. But they said it was important. Very important. I think you should see them now!'

Rick stared at her in amazement, but her eyes refused to meet his. 'Lucy!' he chided, 'there's a dozen other folks out there waiting their turn. Just tell these people to join the queue. They'll have to wait, same as everyone else.' And he turned back to look at the cat.

'What's so special about them anyway, for heaven's sake?' he grumbled, then heard the footsteps. A big man stood framed in the doorway. He wore a heavy plaid jacket. Daniels, the rancher! Rick recognized him immediately.

There was an awkward silence. Another man pushed into the room behind him. It was Mel, the ranch foreman. He was almost as tall as Daniels, but rangy in build. Rumour had it that he was not popular with the other ranch hands.

Rick looked from one to the other, his annoyance giving way to genuine concern. Quickly, he recalled his last visit to the ranch. 'What's wrong?' he asked. 'You got problems?' The old lady slipped quietly out. Mel closed the door behind her.

Daniels came towards him. 'Heard your wife did a good job on that mare at the Freiberg's farm the other day,' he said.

Surprised, Rick smiled. 'Well, thanks. But tell her yourself if you like. She's downstairs in the hospital.'

Mel picked up a small, white pillbox and studied the label. 'Looking after all those cute little pets you got down there,' he drawled. 'Real kind!'

Rick's smile faded. Daniels bent towards him. His breath smelt of tobacco. 'I hear you got a real live timber wolf on these premises, Mister Viccary.'

Rick was taken aback. 'Yes! Yes, I have,' he said uncertainly.

Mel smiled brightly. 'So we've come to free you of all that responsibility.'

'What responsibility?' Rick demanded.

'For harbouring the most evil cattle-killer known to man,' Daniels grated.

Rick's jaw dropped. He took a step backwards and looked from one to the other. 'Look! I'm not hearing this properly! What are you guys saying?'

Daniels glared at him. 'I'm taking that wolf out of here before it does any more damage.'

'What damage?' Rick began, but the rancher ignored him. He pointed to a syringe lying nearby.

'Give it a shot of tranquillizer and we'll be on our way.'

'You can itemize it on your next bill,' Mel sniggered.

Rick went bright red. 'Now you listen to me!' he snapped. 'You can't come in here telling me what I can or cannot do!'

Daniels studied him slowly. His expression hardened. 'You telling me, Viccary, that you're nursing a wolf back to health?' His voice rose. 'So it can go back and kill my stock! You're crazy!'

'No one helps a wolf. Ever!' said Mel, rubbing his knuckles. 'Not if they've any sense.'

'So, hand it over!' Daniels ordered. 'Now!'

Rick could hear Amy laughing and talking with someone downstairs. Her gaiety hung in the silence between them. He swallowed. The men stared at him, waiting. He could feel his hands shaking. He stuffed them in his pockets and took a deep breath. 'Mr Daniels,' he said as evenly as he could, 'I'm a vet. My job is to help animals.

Whatever they might be. That wolf is staying right here!'

Suddenly, Rick's anger boiled over. He pushed past the rancher and flung open the door. 'This is my surgery!' he told them. 'And I've got a lot of people to see!'

Amy was coming up the stairs. He saw the expression on her face. 'These gentlemen are just leaving,' he told her, with heavy emphasis.

Daniels glanced at Amy. 'Maybe I'll give my old friend Ernie Price a phone call,' he told her. 'Just to make sure he's enjoying his vacation.'

The people in the waiting room stared, wide-eyed, as the two men stalked out. In the silence that followed the slamming of the door, they heard the rancher's truck start up and roar away. A smell of exhaust drifted in. Then Amy came bustling back to see them. 'Who's next?' she asked, with a brittle smile.

Twelve

Marak lay motionless, pretending to be asleep. His eyes were closed and his breathing regular. In reality, he was wide awake, absorbing everything around him. The worst of the fever had gone, although he was still weak. All his senses and intelligence were now focused on only one thing – escape!

He listened to the other animals around him, trying to glean any useful information. Some were in pain, others just bored. The dog opposite seemed perfectly content. It had no fear at all of the wolf and this puzzled Marak. He wondered if this was because it belonged to a human.

The smell of humans was everywhere. In the air, along the bars of the cage and on the ground beside him. There was no escaping it. It was a sweet, cloying scent that permeated his fur. The more he had tried to clean himself, the worse the taste got. Marak wrinkled his nose in disgust and began scraping his tongue over his teeth. But it was no good. There was no way of getting rid of it.

Frustrated, he got up and banged his head against the bars. It was a pointless thing to do. And he knew it. The only way out was through the long sliding door that ran the length of the cage. But that was locked on the outside with a large padlock. He had spent many hours the night before, trying to knock it clear with his paws.

He heard a heavy clump of footsteps on the stairs and the click of the door opening. Instinctively, the hair along his jaws bristled. He wanted to flee. But there was nowhere to run to. He could only just turn round inside the cage as it was.

He watched the man from between almost closed eyelids. The dog was wagging its tail and whining in delight. Marak heard the slop of water into empty bowls and smelt food. He saw doors open and swing shut, and heard the dull clang of metal bolts shooting home.

Now the human was coming towards him. It was too much to bear. He snarled and tried to back away. But the fever had left him unsteady and slow. At the far end of the cage a grille opened and a hunk of bloody meat fell with a wet thud in front of him. Without a moment's hesitation, Marak began to tear at it.

Thirteen

The telephone call from Florida came just as they were finishing morning surgery. 'It's for you, Rick!' Lucy Smith called from the reception desk. 'It's Mr Price!'

Amy and Rick looked at one another. 'That's quick!' Amy said.

Rick puffed out his cheeks. 'Daniels must have told him.'

'He said he would,' Amy said simply. She bit her lip. 'Take it easy now, Rick. Remember, the soft answer turneth away wrath. And all that stuff.'

Rick nodded, then licked his lips. 'Put him through, Lucy!' he called.

Amy went over to the window. Two squirrels were chasing each other across the parking lot. People were stopping to watch and smiling. She liked this town. She really wanted to stay.

'Hi there, Mr Price! How is Florida?' Rick asked cheerfully.

She listened to him talking. And heard his voice become defensive. She turned and watched him. Rick held the phone out for her to hear. They stooped over it.

The old man's voice was shrill and agitated. '. . . He's my best customer, Rick. You know that! I want that animal out of there, right now. You know what the alternative is. Just do it!'

There was a click and the line went dead.

'This is getting out of hand,' Rick muttered as they drove home.

'But Price can't fire us,' Amy protested. 'We've signed contracts.'

'With a good lawyer he probably could,' Rick said. 'And we can't afford legal fees.'

Amy shook her head. 'Rick! What's happening? What are we going to do?'

Rick banged his fist on the steering wheel. 'It's the principle of it!' he cried. He glanced across at her. 'I mean, I can see Price's point of view. Just!

But – but there's no way I'm going to put that animal down and have him incinerated!' He touched her arm. 'That's what he's telling me to do!'

They drove in silence for the next few minutes, past the town swimming pool and ice hockey rink, alone with their thoughts. 'Well,' said Rick, as they turned into their road, 'we've got until next weekend. He's not back till then. That gives us seven days to come up with something!'

'What are we going to tell the kids?' Amy asked gloomily. 'They'll be home by now.'

'The truth, I guess.' He slammed the car door. 'I'll e-mail those Yellowstone people right away. Tell 'em it's urgent.'

Ed and Jessica listened to the news, wide-eyed in horror, while Amy banged round the kitchen getting lunch ready.

'So why don't we bring the wolf back here?' Ed demanded, taking a pile of plates from her. 'Just till he's ready to be released.'

She shook her head. 'Be sensible, Ed! Where we going to keep him?' She went to the foot of the stairs. 'Rick!' she shouted. 'Lunch!'

Ed looked at his mother's tense face. She refused

60

to meet his gaze. He took a deep breath and persisted. 'But if the wolf's in a cage, it doesn't matter where we keep him!'

'We could put him in the garage,' Jessica interrupted. 'There's lots of room there!'

'Just go and sit down!' Amy told her. 'You too, Ed!'

Rick came downstairs. He pulled out his chair and slumped into it. He rubbed a hand over his face and said gloomily, 'The Yellowstone folks are not too keen on a solitary male. Something to do with their existing breeding cycle.' He gave his wife a lopsided grin. 'They've got some vacancies for vets, though!'

Amy passed him a salad bowl. 'The kids want to bring the wolf back here!'

Rick looked at them and frowned. 'Run that by me again.'

'Can you imagine how the neighbours would react!' said Amy scornfully.

'We'd keep the cage padlocked like it is now,' Ed argued.

'So he couldn't get out,' Jessica insisted excitedly.

'It wouldn't be for long.'

'Amy!' Rick cried, waving them all to be quiet. 'If we kept the wolf on full medication for another week, what do you reckon his chances would be?'

Amy stared at him. 'You mean of surviving back in the wild?'

Rick nodded energetically.

'Well,' she said thoughtfully, 'in theory, pretty good. Some more days on antibiotics and all that raw meat he's been having should set him up fine. They're pretty tough animals, wolves.' Then seeing the look on his face, protested, 'Rick! No! We can't keep him here!' But it was too late.

Rick was on his feet. He seized her by the shoulders. 'Honey! You're right! Of course you are! But this is the perfect solution. Don't you see? He'll be out of the surgery. And we can release him up at the Canadian border in a few more days. This way, we cover all bases! So what do you say?'

Ed and Jessica whooped with excitement.

Amy put her hands to her ears. 'But what if he gets out?'

'How can he?' Rick laughed. 'There's a five centimetre steel padlock keeping him in! The kids are right! The garage is perfect! We'll bring him here after dark. That way there's a chance no one will see.'

'Some hope in this place,' Amy said, but she managed a little smile. Rick's enthusiasm was as irresistible as always.

Jessica put her arms round Rick's waist and hugged him. 'Just don't tell Nurse Lucy where you're taking him to, Daddy,' she warned.

Fourteen

Ed opened his eyes and stared upwards. For a moment he couldn't think where he was. A dog was barking. It sounded very close. Perhaps it had found the wolf's scent? And then he was suddenly wide awake. The wolf! It was here, in this house, just below his room! Of course, he remembered now.

He pushed himself up and looked around. Bright moonlight flooded across the floor from underneath the curtains. He stretched out a hand towards his alarm clock. Two o'clock. The middle of the night. He had fallen into bed, exhausted, only three hours ago. Now he was wide awake again and ready for anything.

They had all gone back to the surgery together. Ed and Jessica had refused to be left out of the action. The wolf was lightly sedated, then Rick and Amy had manhandled the long steel cage up through the surgery and out into the freezing night air. Amy was worried because two cars had driven past slowly as they were lifting it up on to the tailboard of the truck. Everyone was positive, however, that nobody had seen them park outside their garage and unload.

That wretched dog was barking again. Ed guessed it couldn't be coincidence. He swore under his breath and listened with growing unease. His bedroom was immediately above the garage. He swung out of bed and padded over to the window. It opened silently. Yes! The dog was actually there, sniffing around the brickwork and the edges of the garage door.

He had to quieten the animal at all costs. Heaven knows what would happen if the wolf began howling back or something. Then the fat would really be in the fire! He wanted something to throw and remembered that he'd left an apple beside his bed. He took careful aim and hurled it as hard as he could. It hit the dog on the shoulder. The dog almost fell over in shock, then dodged away through the bushes, yelping loudly.

Ed waited, hardly daring to breathe. But no lights

flashed on in the neighbouring houses. No doors or windows opened or banged shut. And none of his family seemed to have heard either. At last, after an age, peace returned.

Ed grinned. He'd tell his parents about the dog in the morning. The wolf hadn't made a sound. That was lucky. He wondered if it was still sedated. Or just too sensible to make a noise. Perhaps it was asleep? He wondered what wolves dreamt about. His grandparents' dog was always dreaming. Why shouldn't a wolf? Did they ever have nightmares? And just what would frighten a wolf?

He also wondered why everyone seemed to hate wolves so much. All through history, people had regarded them as being really evil. In most countries, they had been systematically persecuted and killed, whenever possible. The wolf in the cage downstairs was frightening only because it was so big. But then so were the animals it preyed on.

But a tiger was almost twice that size, yet no one wanted to kill tigers any more. And tigers often ate people. Ed shook his head. It was all very unfair and illogical, like so much in life. He felt a sudden strong pang of compassion for the wolf. It might even be awake at this moment, listening to his footsteps on the floor overhead. Impulsively, Ed decided to go and see.

He slipped silently out on to the landing. The wooden staircase felt cool and slippery under his feet. The bottom stair creaked loudly and he froze for a long moment, waiting to be discovered. But no one heard.

In the kitchen, the refrigerator hummed quietly. The moonlight fell in wide shafts across the door that led to the garage. He took a deep breath, turned the key and stepped inside.

It was pitch black. He could see nothing. He stared helplessly into the darkness, searching for the darker bulk of the cage. He knew instinctively that the wolf was awake and watching him. He swallowed nervously.

It was cold. Much colder than the rest of the house. The concrete floor felt icy. He strained his senses, but there was nothing to see or hear. Just a powerful musty smell. The smell of warm fur and old moose fat. The smell of a wild animal. A warm, pervading scent that grew stronger all the time as if the wolf was out of his cage and silently circling him.

Ed shivered and felt a prickle of fear gather between his shoulder blades. His mouth had gone dry. He closed his eyes and fought back the demons of his imagination. 'Hello, wolf,' he whispered. 'You won't hurt me, will you? Not when we're all trying to get you better?' The words seemed to hang in the air for a long time.

A sense of timelessness engulfed him. He began to feel light-headed, as if he was floating outside his body, looking down on himself and the cage. The wolf was staring at him and he knew for certain that it understood every word he was saying. A new confidence surged inside him.

He didn't know how or why it was happening. That was unimportant. All Ed knew was that he and the wolf, for some brief particle of time, understood something of the other. And that was wonderful.

His eyes were burning. There were tears running down his cheeks. He licked his lips and tasted the salt. He loved this great silent predator as he had never loved any other animal before. 'We won't let them hurt you,' he mumbled. 'I promise.'

Then the tension became suddenly too much. He fumbled for the light switch. The neon strip light flickered on, banishing that strange other world for ever. The wolf was standing looking at him, his head hunched back into his shoulders. He watched the boy with expressionless yellow eyes.

Long after Ed had gone, Marak stood motionless while the boy's scent slowly faded.

Fifteen

The police department came the following evening. A brand new yellow patrol car, with its blue light flashing, drove slowly up the street. It turned into the Viccarys' drive and parked close to the front door. 'They're home,' said the patrolman, switching off the ignition.

Sheriff Hoskins grunted and heaved his bulk out of the car. He paused to pull on a thick pair of mittens. It had been a cold day. He wouldn't be at all surprised if it didn't snow later. With a bit of luck it might be the last storm of the winter.

He looked around and sighed. He did not relish what he had to do. 'Find out what's holding up the Daniels' truck,' he snapped. 'And tell them to get a move on. Let's get this thing over and done with.'

He surveyed the house. The lights were on and the curtains drawn in the downstairs rooms. No one seemed to have heard them arrive. Probably watching TV, he thought. Reluctantly, he headed for the front door.

He was disappointed with the Viccarys. Up until now they had been perfectly good, law-abiding citizens like almost everyone else in Elliott Lake. Good vets too, or so he'd been told. He didn't much like animals himself so he couldn't judge one way or the other. Then they had to go and do something really stupid like this. Putting everyone's backs up.

Sheriff Hoskins shook his head. He had been one of the first to hear about the wolf. Now it was the talk of the whole town. And he had known it had meant trouble right from the start. Silly people. Most newcomers made the same mistake. Especially city folk. It was up to them to fit in with the local way of life. Not the other way round.

Besides, he reflected, no one in their right mind got on the wrong side of Jake Daniels. The sheriff sighed. Now there was this formal complaint against them. And that was something he could not ignore. Not if he wanted to run for sheriff again at the next civic elections.

Another car drew up with a screech of brakes. He recognized the logo on the doors and groaned. A television film crew scrambled out and immediately began strapping on battery belts and lifting out floodlights. Someone must have tipped them off as well. He recognized the interviewer. The station had sent their A team. Well, if it was going to be on Statewide television he'd better act the part.

'Daniels' people will be here in thirty seconds,' the patrolman called.

Hoskins nodded in relief. 'OK. Let's go!' He put a hand on his holster. It shouldn't be necessary, but you never knew these days. He saw a curtain flick open inside the house and a small face look out. Moments later the door opened. Rick Viccary stood there, joined immediately by Amy. Jessica and Ed squeezed past them and watched open-mouthed as the sheriff strode towards them.

'Hi there!' Rick called. 'Is anything wrong?' Then he threw a hand over his eyes in the sudden glare of the floodlights. 'Hey! What's going on?'

The sheriff spoke slowly and deliberately. 'Mr Viccary! I hear you've got a wild animal on this property! A wolf! Am I right?'

'What are these people doing here?' Rick demanded. 'Who sent them?'

'That's a serious offence against the laws of this State . . . sir,' the sheriff went on.

'But sheriff,' Amy said firmly, 'he's in exactly the same cage as the one in the surgery.' She smiled at him. 'He can't get out, I promise you!'

Rick nodded vigorously. 'He's perfectly safe. Totally secure. There's absolutely no need to worry. Come and have a look if you don't believe me.'

'I intend to,' said Hoskins gravely.

'It's got a huge padlock on it,' Jessica told him with a reassuring smile. 'And we keep all the doors locked.'

Ed stared in disbelief at the sheriff. He visualized the wolf pacing up and down, fearfully listening to the commotion outside. A small crowd of inquisitive neighbours was gathering. Ed saw their heads bending conspiratorially as they greeted one another and pointed excitedly at the garage. He saw their mouths opening and heard the word 'wolf' growing louder and louder.

With a sense of everything coming to an end, he followed his father round to the front of the garage. The camera team was already scuttling ahead of them. 'Open up!' Hoskins ordered tersely.

Rick looked at him and then at the television interviewer. He frowned. 'That's what I was going to do.'

Hoskins made an impatient gesture with his head. He was beginning to enjoy himself. He had never been on TV like this before. He stuck his thumbs in the top of his belt and cleared his throat. 'Just get on with it!'

Rick swung the door up on its hinges. It slid back silently. Ed caught a brief glimpse of the wolf, then the television crew was pushing past, the camera whirring. There was a loud gasp from the crowd and one or two cries of fear.

Hoskins knelt down on one knee and peered in at Marak. 'It's a timber wolf all right!' he called in a loud voice. The crowd shrank back.

'Sheriff! Please listen!' said Rick urgently. 'I promise you, we're releasing it next weekend. Three hundred miles from here. Probably more. Can't we talk this over someplace else?'

Hoskins got to his feet, slowly shaking his head. 'Keeping a wild and dangerous animal in a domestic dwelling is a serious offence. Especially a wolf!'

Amy tugged at his arm. 'Look, sheriff,' she pleaded, 'can't we be reasonable? How about if we take him back to the surgery tonight and then release him way out of town, tomorrow?'

Hoskins was growing impatient. 'Mr Price told you to get it out of there and keep it out. You know that perfectly well!' There was a sudden loud shout. They turned and saw Mel, pushing his way through the crowd. He was followed by three other men.

'Right here, sheriff!' Mel called. 'We came just as soon as we got your message. C'mon boys!'

The crowd parted to let them through. 'What's he doing here?' Rick demanded. 'He's got no right to trespass on my property!'

'These people have been sworn in as deputy sheriffs,' Hoskins snapped. 'I've got nowhere to keep the thing so they're taking it back with them.'

'They'll kill it!' Ed shouted. 'Mum, Dad! We've got to stop them!' He tried to force his way to the cage. The patrolman barred his way. Ed lashed out with his fists. The man caught his arm and yanked it up behind his back. Ed gasped in pain.

Rick started forward in protest. The sheriff held up a large warning hand. 'Impeding officers of the court is another serious offence, Mr Viccary. Just take my advice and let these people do what they have to!'

In silence, they watched the men slide thick wooden staves under the cage. 'Lift!' Mel ordered. The cage lurched, the crowd screamed and the camera zoomed in on Marak's snarling jaws. They carried the wolf out at shoulder height to the waiting truck.

The crowd shrank back. A microphone was thrust into Rick's face. 'You've put everyone's safety in danger, Mr Viccary!' the interviewer shouted. 'Shouldn't someone in your position know better?'

Sixteen

The men stood round the cage, drinking coffee and smoking. It was the grey early morning and the lights in the cookhouse still burned brightly. The air was full of the smell of bacon and toasted bread.

Marak's hackles rose as the cookhouse door banged and Mel came clattering down the concrete steps. Marak sensed he was the men's leader. For the past two days, he had watched them obey him and defer to him. His own eyes never left the man's face.

By now, the wolf had a raging thirst. For the last hour before dawn, he had been trying to scoop in some of the old snow that lay just outside the muddy ring that surrounded his cage. He had even tried using his tail to flick some of it back, but without any luck.

Still keeping an eye on Mel, Marak began licking the steel bars in front of him. Seeing this, one of the men threw what was left of his coffee into the cage. Marak cleared it with a quick sweep of his tongue.

'The thing's sure got a thirst,' the man exclaimed.

'Get a bowl from the cook and fill it up,' Mel ordered. When the man came back, Mel took it from him and carefully placed it just beyond the wolf's reach. Then he splashed a handful of water at Marak's head. The men laughed.

A cook appeared and casually began to sweep the top step with a wooden broom. 'Do you want me to feed him?' he called, jerking his thumb at the cage.

'No! You leave him alone till the boss gets back tonight,' Mel told him. 'Understand?'

'He's a fine-looking creature,' the cook said. 'I'll say that for him.'

'Don't let the boss hear you say that, O'Shaugnessy,' Mel scoffed. 'Not if you want to keep your job!' The men laughed dutifully. 'Hey!' Mel shouted. 'Give me that brush a minute.'

He started poking the broom handle between the bars, trying to prod the wolf. But Marak could anticipate every lunge he made and easily avoided them. The wolf's snarls began to excite the men.

They formed a circle, kicking at the sides and corners of the cage behind the wolf's back to distract him. Soon the stink of their breath was everywhere.

Marak saw the anger in Mel's eyes and felt the growing frenzy of his attacks. Patiently he waited . . . until the heel of Mel's boot slipped, momentarily off-balancing him. Marak turned on him, seizing the broom in his jaws and ripping it towards him with a powerful jerk. Mel stumbled and fell forward on to the cage. In an instant, the wolf was slashing at his outstretched fingers. The water bowl went up on its side with a clatter and the men looked on with open mouths.

There was blood on the snow, bright red drops like holly berries. Mel twisted away, rolling on the ground cursing and sucking the ends of his fingers. The brush lay in two splintered halves.

'Goddam wolf!' Mel screamed. The men grinned sheepishly but said nothing. No one attempted to help him up. They shuffled their feet instead and stared at the ground. Mel aimed a kick at the cage. Growling horribly, Marak tried to force his head between the bars desperate to get at the man. Mel jumped backwards in real fear.

'Goddam wolf!' he swore again. Then turning on

the men, shouted, 'OK! OK! Let's get to work!' Obediently they followed him. Soon a vehicle started up, gears clashed as it drove away.

A few minutes later, the cook reappeared. He looked round cautiously then, satisfied, came down the steps carrying a battered tin bowl. It was very full and some of the water splashed over his boots.

Nervously, he pushed it up against the side of the cage with an outstretched arm. Marak could smell fear on the man's skin. Then the cook sat back on his haunches and stared at him. 'And if you're really good, I'll bring you something to eat in a little while,' he promised. He chuckled and got to his feet. Marak waited until the door banged behind him, then turned his head and drank.

Seventeen

Amy stood in the kitchen watching the early morning television news. The weekend's events were still the lead story. Angrily, she switched it off as the children came down for breakfast. Then the telephone rang. It was the editor of the local newspaper. He was sending a reporter and a photographer to interview the Viccarys. Then Rick appeared, looking strained. There was an e-mail from Mr Price. He was cutting short his holiday.

Breakfast was a miserable affair, everyone overwhelmed by what had happened. 'I wish I had never found that wolf,' Amy muttered to Rick, opening the fridge door.

Rick put his arm round her shoulders. 'It's not your fault,' he said quietly. 'And it's not the wolf's either. We did nothing wrong helping that animal. That's our job. But I feel bad about bringing him here.' He ran his fingers through his hair. 'And I'd sure love to know who told the sheriff.'

Amy stared at him. 'You will pretty soon if they take us to court!'

Miserably, Ed and Jessica walked down the road to the bus stop. Jessica greeted her friends with her usual smile, but they pretended to be absorbed in something else. There was an uncomfortable silence. On the bus, even Pete Daniels and his crew ignored them, talking loudly amongst themselves about an ice hockey game they had watched on television the night before.

Ed desperately wanted to find out what was happening to the wolf, but his pride wouldn't let him ask. Besides, he knew the Daniels gang was ignoring him for a reason. Were they goading him into asking, just so they could deny all knowledge? Or did they just want to make him grovel? Well, he wouldn't play along with their squalid little game, let alone give them the satisfaction of seeing how distressed he really was.

At school, the girls seemed to shrink away whenever Ed passed them in the corridors. The elder boys just pretended he wasn't there. Even the teachers seemed unfriendly and distant. Several times, he caught them looking sideways at him.

Gloomily, he wondered how his parents were coping and knew it would be even worse for them. But above all he thought of the wolf and fretted for him. At lunchtime, Jessica found him and they ate at a table by themselves. Ed saw she was close to tears. They walked down to the school gates and back again. 'Have they killed the wolf yet?' she kept asking. 'Has that man killed him?'

There was a lump in Ed's throat that just wouldn't go away. He held her arm tightly. 'I don't know. I just don't know!' And his eyes grew hot. The bell rang and they separated for the afternoon. No one said a word to them, until the school bus pulled up at their stop.

As they were leaving their seats, Pete Daniels suddenly shouted, 'Hey Viccary! Want to know what's happening to your wolf?' He waited, a smirk of triumph on his face. And Ed realized he had planned this moment all day long.

Ed stared at the boy with loathing. He wanted to crush his face between his hands and tear off the smug leer. Instead, he forced himself to wait and listen. He gripped the back of his seat so hard his knuckles felt they were cracking.

Pete's smile grew wider. 'My dad's coming back tonight,' he drawled. 'He wants to take a special look at your wolf. A sort of last look! Know why?' He looked round at his friends. Someone giggled. ' 'Cos Mel's gonna shoot it dead tomorrow breakfast time! So how does that grab you . . . Bunny Hugger!'

The boys on the seat beside him laughed and catcalled. Ed looked at Daniels' grinning red face, and his own misery, helplessness and humiliation boiled over. He hurled himself at Daniels.

The bus driver eventually separated the struggling mass of boys. She dragged Ed clear. 'Young man, I'm going to report you to the Principal directly I get back.' She peered at him more closely. 'You're the Viccary boy, aren't you?' There was dislike in her voice.

Ed and Jessica walked back towards their house. 'Did Pete Daniels really mean all that?' she asked in a small, trembling voice. Ed nodded. Jessica had fought back tears all day long at school out of sheer pride. But now there seemed no point. 'It's like a bad dream,' she sobbed. 'And there's nothing we can do. Or Mum or Dad.'

84

Ed only half heard her. He was remembering the way the wolf had looked at him while the men were dumping his cage into their truck.

'Where's the key for that padlock?' he asked suddenly.

Jessica wiped her eyes on her coat sleeve. 'In the kitchen. On the hook with the spare car keys. Why?'

Ed shook his head. 'Nothing. Just a crazy idea,' he said vaguely and put an arm round her shoulders to cover his excitement.

'Come on,' he said encouragingly. 'Let's see how the folks got on!'

Eighteen

The town clock chimed midnight. Ed counted the strokes. He looked up at his parents' bedroom window but no one seemed to have heard the back door closing behind him. He let his breath out slowly in relief. It formed a long silvery plume on the night air.

It was time to go. For a moment he was tempted to creep back to his warm bed and pull the duvet over his head. Nobody would ever know he had chickened out. Not the wolf. Not Jessica. Not his parents. Only himself.

Instead, he pushed his mountain bike down to the road, had a last look back, then pulled his baseball cap hard down on his head. The next moment he was moving smoothly in and out of the streetlights, accelerating all the time.

Outside the town, he swung off on to an old gravel road, still bumpy with uncleared patches of snow. He cycled hard for twenty minutes, then saw the flash of approaching headlights. He skidded to a halt beside a clump of bushes and threw the bike down. He lay full-length on the ground, hiding his face in his hands.

The car rushed past, its radio blaring. Ed watched the tail lights until they were out of sight. Then he took off a glove and patted his pocket. Reassured, he mounted the bike and pedalled on. Ten minutes later, a couple of lights appeared some way off the road. It had to be the ranch. His father had been called out there a month ago and Ed had gone with him out of curiosity. He looked for the turning.

Fifty metres short of a long wooden gate, he dismounted. As he did so, the moon came out and it was suddenly just like daylight. Ed froze, feeling as conspicuous as a fly on a whitewashed ceiling. An owl shrieked just above his head and he bit his tongue. He stood stock-still, his heart thumping madly.

The seconds slowly ticked by. Cautiously, he began to relax. Nothing else seemed to be stirring. He noticed a large fir tree set apart from the others. A good place to leave the bicycle.

He waited until the moon slipped behind a cloud, then bent double and ran forward. A wooden rail circled round the front of the ranch. Ed crouched beside it and got his bearings. Yes! He remembered it all now. There was the Daniels' house with its outside porch. Beyond it were the barns and the stables and all the other outbuildings where the men lived and slept. The wolf was somewhere in there.

There was sweat running into his eyes. He brushed it away. Not really surprised. This was no longer a game. If he was caught there would be huge trouble. All his family would suffer. He took a deep breath and ducked under the railing. Now he really was in enemy territory.

He thrust the thought away from him. This was no time for play-acting. The wolf's life depended on his keeping a cool head. He ran towards a long, low building and reached it just as the moon reappeared. He waited in the shadows while he got his breath. There was a large car parked nearby, and he recognized it. Daringly he stole out and touched the bonnet. It was still warm.

So the rancher was back home. He began to sidle

along the building, taking great care to stay inside the shadows. He reached the end. Taking a deep breath, he peered round the corner. And almost yelled in fright! A man stood there in the open, barely five metres away. His shadow stretching across the ground towards the boy. Ed's eyes bulged in horror.

There was a sudden sharp click. A lighter flared. Followed by a loud cough. And Mel turned and walked straight towards him!

Ed's eyes snapped shut. This was the end. There was no time to run. And nowhere to run to. He stood shaking with fear, waiting to be discovered, while Mel's boots crunched towards him over the frosty ground. The man coughed again and turned his head to spit. He strode past the boy close enough to touch, still clearing his throat.

Ed's heart stood still. He waited, petrified, for the man to hesitate and look back, for his shout of surprise. Then a door opened and an outside light came on.

'Thanks for coming!' called Daniels, from twenty metres away. 'Mary Jane's in a state. She wants it over and done with right away. I was just looking out some ammunition.' The door closed with a bang and the voices died away.

Ed clung to the corner of the building, sweat pouring off him. They were just about to shoot the wolf. And he didn't even know where the animal was. He began to run. Nothing mattered now. Only finding that cage. There was no time left for caution. He stumbled across the yard peering at the buildings, staring into the shadows. Trying to remember where he had gone with his father.

He ran past a large hut and heard sleepy voices inside. There was an outside light burning at the far end. The bunkhouse. Which meant that the building beside it was the cookhouse. And the stables, he recalled, were in the darkness somewhere behind. Then his foot slipped on a patch of ice and he went full-length.

It was like hitting concrete. He couldn't move. Or breathe. Winded. And helpless. His bones were dissolving in a sea of pain. If Mel found him now . . .

An age went by before he managed to push himself back up on to his hands and knees. He sucked in lungfuls of air, groaning as he did so. The moon came out. He cursed it and looked away. And saw the cage!

He staggered towards it, his hands fumbling for the key. Where was it? He heard the sound of a door closing and voices coming from the direction of the main house. Daniels! And Mel. With a gun! His stomach heaved. Bile filled his mouth and trickled down his chin.

But with another part of his brain he found the key and coolly fitted it into the padlock. Two deliberate turns and the lock sprang open. He twisted it clear and threw it as far away from him as he could. The wolf stood motionless. The boy bent over the cage and began tugging back the sliding door. It started to move then stuck. He tried again. It was buckled!

Sobbing with rage, Ed kicked it. The door jerked back a couple more centimetres. He kicked again and again. The wolf was forcing his head through the opening. Ed flung himself at the door and the wolf's fur was suddenly thick in his face. The scent overpowering.

He had a confused memory of a huge head pushing him aside and a hard body streaming past. Then he was sitting up and staring at the wolf towering over him, its jaws only centimetres from his face. Their eyes met in a long stare.

Mel was coughing again, very close now. The wolf seemed to hesitate, then quickly licked the boy's hand and was gone. Racing for the shadows and away into the night. Ed scrambled up, his heart singing in triumph, and pelted after him.

There was shouting and confusion behind him. Doors slamming and lights flashing on. In a daze, Ed bent low over the handlebars and pedalled furiously. He had lost his baseball cap and couldn't remember when. He looked back over his shoulder but there was no sign of any pursuit. The drumming of the tyres rose like a great shout of triumph inside his head. He had done it! He had freed the wolf. Nothing would ever matter again!

Nineteen

Deep in the shadows of an ancient redwood, a female wood mouse stood rigid with fear as Marak bounded past into the night. Four hours ago she had given birth to six helpless, pink babies. They were her first litter. Now she was hungry and needed to feed. They had squeaked in protest as she got to her feet, shaking them off. She left the snug, moss-lined nest behind her and scurried upwards into the moonlight.

When the wolf had gone, she clambered up on to a massive tree root and looked around. Forty metres above, an old grey owl dipped a wing and silently circled the tree. He watched the wolf until it disappeared amongst the trees further up the hillside.

The mouse ran along the tree root. The owl heard the faint scratching of her claws and his head swung down. Two huge fierce eyes gleamed in concentration as he came swooping towards her, talons opening.

He took the mouse up on to his favourite branch and ripped her open with one stab of his beak. Then he swallowed her shaking his head vigorously as he did so. On the ground below, Marak's footprints glistened in the frost.

At the top of the hill, Marak stopped and looked back. The men's voices rose on the still, cold air like a swarm of angry bees. Marak listened to their anger and a wild elation seized him. He was free! The cage was gone! He felt strong and fit. No man would ever catch him again. He was free!

He yelped in happiness and threw himself on his back, rolling around in the snow like a puppy. He caught the end of his tail between his teeth and chased round and round, splattering snow in all directions. He pounced on a thin, brittle stick and shredded the bark between his teeth. Then he sat down, put his head back and howled in triumph.

Down beside the cookhouse, Daniels shouted for silence. The men listened to the wolf's howl, open mouthed. Then they cursed and shouted back at the wolf at the tops of their voices. Enraged, the rancher fired his rifle at the distant trees.

Marak heard the sudden, sharp crack and understood. Memories came flooding back. He remembered Claw and the yearlings, their bodies convulsing beside him on the ice. That sound meant life and death. He would never forget it.

There was another shot. He flinched as the bullet screamed overhead. It was time to leave this place. He howled again, this time mocking the men. The next moment, he was racing down the far side of the hill, following the path the moonlight made.

The sound of the men's voices died away. Soon, there was only himself and the sweet taste of the air. He ran north back towards his old territory. Every atom of his being urging him onwards.

Twenty

'Ed! For heaven's sake! Get up! You're going to be late for school!' Amy Viccary shook her son's shoulder.

Later, at breakfast, she stared at him and said critically, 'You all right? You look like you didn't get much sleep.'

Rick frowned. 'We're all worried, Ed, but you musn't miss your sleep. Life's got to go on.'

Jessica said nothing. She was puzzled. She studied her brother over a spoonful of cereal. She knew Ed well. Something had happened, she decided. Something he didn't want their parents to know. Well, he'd tell her, she thought philosophically. He always did in the end.

As they left the house together, Ed caught sight of

himself in the hall mirror. There were black shadows under his eyes while the rest of his face looked drawn. He grinned at the reflection. He couldn't care less!

His heart sang all the way to the bus stop. He could hardly believe it was true. He had done it! It was the most fantastic feeling of his life. He wanted to sing and shout and tell everyone that the wolf was free. By now, it would be miles away. And the wolf had known it was him! He was sure of it. He walked on air, a grin spreading over his face.

Jessica stared at him and frowned. What was there to smile about, she wondered? 'Ed! What's happened? What have you done?'

Ed looked up at the sky. 'I'll tell you after school.'

She stopped dead, searching his face for clues. 'Oh, come on! Why not now? What's so important?'

He laughed. 'Important? It's just fantastic! I can't even talk about it. Not yet!'

Her heart leapt. 'Is it about the wolf?'

He punched the air. 'Ed!' she cried, running round in front of him. 'What's happened? Ed! Tell me!'

He put a finger to his lips and shook his head. 'I'll

tell you later. I promise. But, you're not to say a word until then. It's our secret. Understand?'

As the bus drew up, it was all Ed could do not to start dancing. He had to keep biting his tongue all the way to his seat. He wanted to laugh and cheer and grab Pete Daniels by his little piggy ears and twist them off. One thing was for sure. He'd never take any more stick from any of them again.

Pete Daniels looked sullen. He didn't say a word until the bus turned in through the school gates. Then he kicked the back of Ed's seat and shouted, 'Hey! City boy! My dad shot your wolf last night. Hope you're good at cleaning out cages!' The others sniggered.

Ed had been waiting for this moment. He was going to enjoy it. He got up and surveyed them coolly, and laughed. He couldn't help it. 'You're full of it, Daniels! Just full. And you're so stupid you can't even lie properly.' He studied the boy's uncomprehending face. Then he reached down and tweaked his nose. 'Get a life, Hayseed,' he grinned. 'You bore me!'

And with that, he walked down the bus and out into the bright spring sunshine.

Later that day, Ed told Jessica. They walked to a

little park not far from their house. It was empty, except for a pair of crows who put their heads on one side, and examined them with beady eyes. Ed pointed to some nearby swings.

They sat side by side, gently moving to and fro. Someone had been clearing the snow away. It lay in dirty piles close by. Ed took a deep breath and told her what he had done.

'That's wonderful! That's fantastic!' she interrupted him, jumping down and flinging her arms around him. 'Ed, you're so brave! You're unbelievable! Come on! Let's tell Mum and Dad right away!' And she began tugging at his hand.

He caught her by the arm and pulled her back. 'No, Jess! They mustn't know!'

She tried to wriggle away from him. 'Come on! Let's go home!'

Ed held her until she became cross with him. 'But why not?' she demanded. 'Why can't we tell them? They'll be so proud of you.'

'The less Mum and Dad know, the better,' he insisted. 'That way, they'll be telling the truth when they get asked. And people like the sheriff or Mr Price will believe them.'

He looked down at her, his face suddenly serious.

'Jess! Listen! If the folks knew I had done it, they'd come clean and tell everyone. You know how honest they are.' He shook his head. 'Mum and Dad are in big enough trouble as it is. You don't want them getting the sack, do you?'

She shook her head unhappily. Then a terrible thought struck her. 'But what if someone saw you? And what happens when they do find out it was you? They'll expel you!' She put her hand to her mouth in horror. 'Perhaps they know already! Didn't you see all those funny looks we got at school today? Oh Ed! You idiot!'

'No one saw me. Listen Jess. I'll tell Mum and Dad, I promise. But not now. Later. In the holidays. When all the fuss dies down.'

She stood irresolute. 'What happens if the wolf stays round here?'

'It won't. It'll never come back. Would you?'

She thought about it for a moment, then reluctantly agreed. 'I'm just worried about Mum and Dad. And you – and – all of us.'

He stood up. 'We just stay cool. Really cool. That way we win everything.'

She looked at him, wanting to believe him. 'OK,' she said at last. 'But be very careful at school. Don't say anything at all to Pete Daniels or anyone. Whatever they say or do to you. Promise me?'

He grinned and gently punched her arm. 'Hey! What about the wolf then? We beat 'em, didn't we? All of them!'

Twenty-one

For the next three nights, Marak made his way through the mountains. He ran at a steady lope, his great paws gripping the snow effortlessly, powering him on.

He skirted round the highest peaks, unerringly picking his way over fallen trees and through the dense underbrush of the forest floor. And all the time, he followed the invisible track that would take him home.

He slept during the day curled up like a dog, happy to lie out in the open. Spring was coming early that year. Already the sun felt hot on his back. He slept soundly, hardly moving, in a deep, dreamless sleep. Yet one part of his brain always remained alert, listening for any sign of danger.

The days grew longer and the forest came alive with new sounds. Bird song, tentative at first, swelled as the sun climbed higher into cloudless skies. Insects hummed. Long icicles dribbled away into nothing. The ground steamed in the midday heat. And Marak listened to the squirrels squabbling and remembered he was hungry.

He sat up, looked around and yawned. Then he scratched. It was a long, luxurious scratch and he closed his eyes in pleasure until it was over. That done, he set out to find something to eat. The past few days had already taught him that hunting on his own was not easy. It was a thing he had never had to do. Before, there had always been the pack. Ironically, the woods here were full of prey.

Yesterday, he had found caribou trails and seen a small herd of white-tailed deer, grazing amongst the trees. Crawling after them on his belly, he had stalked them for most of the morning. Then a jay saw him and screamed a warning, its harsh cry panicking the herd.

Furious, Marak broke cover and leapt after them. The deer immediately fanned out in all directions and he hesitated a moment too long, uncertain which one to chase. But by then they were safe, dodging between the trees and outrunning him. He had stood and watched them go, listening to the jay cackling in spite. Afterwards the bird followed him, flying from tree to tree, mocking him. In the end he had turned and slunk away.

It would have been so different if the rest of the pack had been there. He knew how to deal with jays. He played dead and it worked every time. It was a trick he had seen his own father do. While the pack spread out to encircle their prey, Marak would suddenly slump to the ground and lie there motionless. The bird, thinking he was dead, would become delirious with delight. Its screams of triumph would distract the deer and hold their attention long enough for the rest of the pack to surround them.

Marak remembered the jay and grew angry. He snarled and looked around. There was a flutter of wings in the bushes ahead and he stopped in disbelief. The jay greeted him with a loud shriek and landed on a branch directly above his head.

Marak sprang at the bird and almost caught it, his teeth snapping just short of the jay's tail feathers. The bird screamed in terror and flew to the top of the highest tree, scolding and complaining. Marak's head drooped. Every animal within a half mile would have already heard it and been warned. There was no point staying here any longer.

He was luckier later that night. He stopped on top of a steep cliff and looked out over a wide, treeless plain. The ground was broken by deep ravines and littered with huge outcrops of rock, stained like old teeth. There was no snow to be seen.

It was not easy picking his way down. The rocks were jagged and hurt his feet. Loose stones rattled down in front of him in miniature avalanches. He was tired, bad-tempered and very hungry by the time he finally jumped down on to level ground.

He stopped to listen. Almost at once he heard the sound of paws scraping together. His head went up as he listened. The animal was stationary. No more than a hundred metres away. It was a soft, almost gentle sound.

Puzzled, he stole forward. The sound of scraping became more insistent. He heard a squeal and a spasm of hunger squeezed his empty stomach. There was a pile of rocks in front of him and he knew the animal was there.

He began to run, his eyes gleaming and his mouth filling with saliva. All his senses concentrating on the next few seconds. Then he was brushing past the rocks, spinning round and leaping towards the pair of mating hares. Their high-pitched screams abruptly muffled as he crashed down on top of them. He ate them greedily leaving only their paws and some splinters of bone for the coyotes.

Afterwards, he howled for twenty minutes into the vastness of the plain. But there was no answering call. No other pack challenged him. No solitary wolf howled back in sympathy. He was alone in a land empty of his own kind.

He ran on for another couple of miles. But by then, the sky was turning grey over the eastern horizon and he knew dawn was not far away. He found a long, overhanging rock at the top of a steep gully and squeezed in underneath. It made a perfect hiding place. He listened carefully for a while, then closed his eyes.

Twenty-two

It was not a meeting Mr Price was looking forward to. As he drove up to the Daniels' ranch, he saw them waiting for him in the yard. He was evidently not going to be offered a cup of coffee.

He clambered out of his car and shook hands with both men.

'Thanks for coming, Ernie!' Daniels said. 'So, what have you got for me?'

The old man shuffled his feet. 'Well, the Viccarys say they didn't do it,' he began.

Mel laughed. 'Surprise, surprise!'

Price ignored him. 'I've interviewed both of them. On their own and together. The Viccarys swear on everything they hold dear, they know nothing about it.'

'Well, they would, wouldn't they,' Daniels interrupted.

'They say they didn't open the cage,' the vet continued. 'And that they never came anywhere near your place.' He avoided the rancher's stare.

Daniels said nothing for a moment. He studied the old man's face, then asked quietly, 'And you believe them?'

Price rubbed a hand over his brow. 'I don't know what to believe.' He closed his eyes. 'Jake, I just don't know!'

'They had the key! Or are they denying that as well?'

A drop of perspiration ran down the back of Price's neck. 'No. They admit it's gone. They just say it wasn't them that let the wolf go. Oh, for heaven's sake!'

'You're too nice,' Daniels remarked, breaking the silence. 'Always were.'

Price looked at him. 'They're good vets. Both of them.' He thought for a moment, choosing his words carefully. 'We all make mistakes . . .' he began.

Daniels' face darkened. 'I admire your loyalty, Ernie. But don't you go around saying that sort of thing too often. Some of your other clients might not be as understanding as me.'

Price bit his lip.

Mel cleared his throat, and spat expertly at a nearby post.

'Just remind me, will you,' asked Daniels, briskly, 'what sort of employment contract you got the Viccarys on?'

'A year,' the vet told him. 'Both of them. There's six more months to go.'

Daniels traced a pattern in the dust with the toe of his boot. 'Here's something else that's worrying me, Ernie. Those charges the sheriff's bringing against the Viccarys. You given that much thought?' He stared hard at the old man.

Price licked his lips.

'Only, I can just picture busloads of those animal rights crazies coming out here and protesting and making trouble for everyone.' The rancher was no longer smiling. 'And all those television cameras outside the courthouse. Bad for the town. Bad for business. Especially yours!'

The old man's shoulders sagged.

Daniels put his arm round the vet and led him back towards his car. 'So, what do you say, Ernie? Would you like me to have a talk with the sheriff?' He opened the car door. 'Just to see if there's any way round this problem? 'He leaned through the open window. 'After all, it won't be much fun for the Viccarys either, living in a town where no one wants them! What do you say?'

They watched the car drive away. 'Now that's what I call a good morning's work!' said Mel, with satisfaction.

Twenty-three

Marak's eyes flicked open. Something had woken him. But what? He lay motionless. There was something wrong. His ears pricked forward. The ground in front of him was bathed in bright sunlight. He could feel the heat reflecting upwards from the creamy-coloured rock.

He watched a butterfly flutter past and land on a patch of sand. It spread its wings revelling in the warmth. It looked like a tiny patch of fresh blood. Marak stared at it and heard the sound again. A thin hissing sound.

The hair on his neck bristled. It was coming from somewhere in front of him. A menacing noise. He must get out from under this rock. And fast! Then he could face whatever it was. As he dragged himself backwards, the butterfly danced away.

He stared into the gully, knowing the sound came from down there. Cautiously, he moved forwards, his nose just above the ground. There was a sudden loud rattle beside him. He had a fleeting glimpse of a wide-open pink mouth, then the snake struck.

Its head thudded into his side, the fangs biting deep into the thick fur. For a split second, Marak stared down into a pair of expressionless black eyes. Then the wolf was up on his hind legs, boxing the snake away, yelping in shock.

The rattlesnake dropped back to the ground. For a fleeting instant its head lay motionless on the sand, extended and helpless. Then with a strong rippling movement, it coiled back and reared up.

Marak saw the long white fangs and the darting tongue. He snarled at it and started barking. The snake's head swayed, following his movements. Its eyes fixed hypnotically on his own. He made a sudden feint with a paw. The snake hissed and the end of its tail became a frenzied rattle.

The snake struck in a blur of movement. Too quick for the wolf to follow. It hit him low on the shoulder, its head half hidden in Marak's coat. Marak felt its mouth, twisting from side to side, trying to penetrate his fur. He leapt sideways in fear and disgust and remembered the snake's vulnerability. In that briefest of moments, while the snake lay inert at the end of its strike, a heavy paw thudded down and pinned its head to the ground.

The snake writhed. Its rattle came whipping up into Marak's face jabbing him in the eye. He flinched and yanked his head away. But he kept his paw firmly anchored on the rattler's head. The snake threshed from side to side. Marak bent down and bit straight through the backbone.

The rattler's body convulsed. It gripped his leg in fury, wrapping itself around him. He could feel the muscles pulsating along the length of its body. It was much heavier than he had expected. Then the head jerked free from under his paw and stretched towards him. Marak saw venom bubbling at the end of its fangs. He panicked, leaping off to one side and finding it still coiled around his leg!

He raked at it with his free foot, his claws tearing deep furrows down its back. The snake struck at him. Once! Twice! Then the rattler's grasp faltered. Slowly, it began to slip back to the ground, still hissing loudly. It lay in the dust, its body flailing on either side of its crushed back. Its movements became erratic. Soon they stopped altogether.

Marak watched it die. He was panting hard and shaking. There were two separate streams of venom running down the front of his leg. He sat down and watched the poison begin to drip, snail-like, on to his paw.

After a while, he walked around the rattlesnake carefully studying its markings. It was the biggest one he had ever seen. Two metres long and as thick as a rat for most of its length. The rattle intrigued him. He prodded it a couple of times but, getting no response, left the snake lying there. The buzzards would soon find it. He looked down into the gully and heard the sound of hissing again.

Marak hesitated, but in the end his curiosity drove him on. He edged forwards, taking great care to scan the rocks and stones in front of him before he took each new step. The hissing was continuous and getting louder all the time. He shivered.

He stared at the ground along the bottom of the gully. And saw it moving! The next moment he realized it was alive with snakes. Hundreds of them were slithering, entwining, flowing in and out of a hissing carpet of other snakes, all waking from their long hibernation.

Marak watched, mesmerized, hardly daring to breathe. Terrified in case they heard him. Fascinated, he stared at the snakes and slowly realized the carpet was moving towards him. He took a step backwards. And another.

Then his nerve broke. He spun round and ran whining like a cub back up the path into the world beyond.

Twenty-four

Amy and Rick belonged to the town choir. It met every Tuesday evening in the local leisure centre. The two of them drove there after supper, in good time to meet friends before the rehearsal began.

That night, Rick was sitting on a corner of the stage, his legs dangling, idly looking out over the room. People intrigued him and he derived a great deal of pleasure from watching them.

He saw Amy walking towards a small group. She had a nice smile, he thought, and she smiled a lot. He also noticed something else. As Amy approached, the people in the group all turned towards each other and stood closer together. Amy paused in confusion, her cheerful greetings breaking against the wall of their backs. It all happened so quickly, Rick wondered if he had been dreaming.

But it happened again. And shortly afterwards, for a third time. His jaw dropped. There was no mistaking it. They were ignoring her. Why? Horrified, he watched her go up to a woman standing on her own. Rick knew her by sight. She and her husband kept the hardware store in town. The woman gave Amy a tight little smile and the next moment, was walking away to join someone else. Amy hesitated and blushed scarlet with embarrassment.

Rick's heart went out to her. He jumped down off the stage and hurried towards her. But just then, someone clapped their hands and announced that it was time to begin.

Driving back later that evening, he looked across at her. Amy's face was set in a frozen smile. He touched the side of her cheek.

Amy's eyes glistened. She blinked quickly then smiled back.

Twenty-five

All that day, the wolf ran northwards across the badlands. He loped effortlessly across the silent expanse of rock and sand, while gritty dust clogged his nostrils and furred his tongue. He only saw one other animal. A half-starved coyote, which followed him at a respectful distance to the boundaries of its own territory, then disappeared.

He stopped once in the early afternoon beside a rocky outcrop. He scrambled upwards, working his way between the boulders until he stood against the skyline. He looked around carefully, first glancing back for any sign of pursuit.

When he was satisfied there were no men following him, he turned and studied the land in front. He saw a line of bulky shadows strung out along the horizon. A pair of eagles swung slowly above them, rising effortlessly in the thermals. Marak swished his tail in delight. He knew those hills. He remembered their shapes. His old territory lay not far behind them. He would be there before dawn!

Eagerly, he scrambled back down, sliding the last five metres on his haunches in a sudden rush of small stones. He saw a large lizard sunning itself on a rock and leapt at it. But the lizard had darted to safety long before Marak's teeth closed with a snap. Lizards fascinated Marak. As a cub, his mother had brought him a dead one to play with. It had intrigued him even then and he had spent many hours since, trying to catch one.

Cheerfully, he set off towards the distant hills. He ran quickly and reached them just after dusk. It was like entering a new world. The air was full of the heady scent of pine resin. He filled his lungs with it and for a moment felt giddy. The ground was soft and cool under his paws and he stood quite still, savouring the sensation.

He found a stream where the water tumbled green from the melting ice. He drank greedily until his stomach grew bloated. He turned away and walked until he could no longer hear the rush of water. He listened for a little while longer, then dropped down and slept for an hour. Then he went hunting.

It was a perfect night. The air was warm and full of scents. The woods were alive with sound. Marak stood perfectly still, absorbing the information all around him. He heard the terrified shriek of a squirrel and saw the branch of a fir tree dip and sway. The squirrel fled across a patch of open ground. Then it was leaping into the branches of another tree and racing upwards. Marak caught the scent of a weasel. A moment later he saw it, following remorselessly, its little red eyes gleaming in anticipation.

But by then he had found a scent that drove everything else from his mind. It was very faint. He turned his head from side to side trying to pinpoint where it had come from. Satisfied, he began to follow. Half a mile further on, at the head of a long shallow valley, he found the caribou's trail.

Eagerly, Marak examined the hoof marks. They were almost twenty centimetres across and had sliced deep into the wet earth. Water had seeped into the footprints so that by now they were almost a quarter full.

Experimentally, Marak put his weight on a front paw and studied the way the water oozed out from underneath.

The caribou, he decided, had been here about nightfall. He also noticed the long scrape marks behind each hoof print. At first, this puzzled him. Then he realized he was tracking a solitary bull.

Every year at this time, female caribou gathered in huge numbers, forming their own herds. They then made their way north through these hills and on to the tundra, hundreds of miles beyond. The entire herd would then drop their calves over a three-day period to confuse predators. There was safety in numbers.

Marak examined its tracks thoughtfully. A bull this size would be a challenge for an entire wolf pack. But this one was plainly exhausted and dragging its feet. Worn out either from the long winter or from protecting its harem during the rutting season.

It might be wounded or incapacitated after battling with other males. Whatever the reason, it was now weak. There was always a chance Marak might catch it unawares. He began to run, following the scent and thinking hard.

Twenty minutes later he found a large patch of blueberries. The bull had stopped here to graze. The tracks were much fresher and Marak knew the caribou was not far ahead. The valley began to open out. Dense woods giving way to small meadows interspersed with stands of trees.

And all the time, Marak's hunger grew. A caribou this size would feed a whole pack for a week. He ran faster, the thought of fresh meat filling his senses. There was a large copse ahead. Marak guessed that the caribou would circle round it rather than waste energy pushing through. He slipped between the trees and jumped over the tangles of brushwood, heading for the far side.

He knew it wouldn't be long now before he caught sight of the animal. He was relishing the thought when a sudden scent, a terrifying scent, brought him to a skidding halt. There were only two animals in the world that frightened Marak. One of them was a human – the other was a full-grown grizzly bear.

Twenty-six

Slowly, carefully, Marak eased his way forward, every muscle tensed for instant flight. His eyes scanned the undergrowth searching for any sign of the bear. He had met grizzlies before. He knew just what they were capable of.

He had seen an enraged female rip the head off a fully-grown wolf who had come too close to her cub. One swipe of her paw, with its ten-centimetre-long claws, had killed the wolf stone dead. While the rest of the pack howled in rage, the grizzly had even picked up the carcass and carried it off with her. The pack had followed for a mile, snarling and threatening, but had scattered when a male bear came running up.

Marak remembered that now. Nervously, he kept

glancing back over his shoulder. Grizzlies were expert stalkers and cunning hunters. Despite their size, they could move silently when they needed to. They could also run as fast as a wolf, in quick bursts. Marak knew he had to get out of this wood as fast as he could. If the grizzly charged at this short range, he would be in deadly danger.

He reached the edge of the wood and froze, one paw still poised in mid-air. The rank smell of grizzly was suddenly overpowering. It clung to the bushes on either side. It lay heavily across the ground in front of him. It was a sour smell, full of warning. The bear had been here very recently. Perhaps in the last few minutes!

There was a sudden commotion in the branches above his head. A night hawk screeched in triumph. Marak peered up, startled by the noise. A thrush's egg landed on the ground beside him and cracked open. While the parent birds beat at the hawk with outstretched wings, Marak licked up the egg and slipped into the open.

Fifty metres further on, he picked up the caribou's trail and knew the grizzly was there before him. Marak snarled bad-temperedly. This changed everything. If the grizzly brought down the bull caribou, it would stay with its kill for days. Most grizzlies even slept on top of their prey to deny any other predator a free meal.

A well-led wolf pack could sometimes find a way of distracting a grizzly. Marak had done it several times by approaching suicidally close. While the bear chased after him, the rest of the pack had raced in and torn chunks of meat from the carcass. But that was impossible now he was on his own.

With a shock, he realized he had been slavishly following the caribou's tracks. He couldn't believe his stupidity. The grizzly had only to look back to see him coming. After that, it would be all too easy to lay an ambush. This was not the way to survive.

A little later, he smelt water. Soon afterwards, he heard it splashing over stones. At the same moment, he caught his first sight of the caribou. It was not more than five hundred metres away. It was drinking. Its front legs splayed out on either side of its head.

Something moved at the edge of Marak's vision. He glanced round and his eyes widened. One hundred metres behind the caribou, a huge grizzly charged out of a clump of bushes, racing on all four legs towards it.

The caribou drank greedily, oblivious to everything. The rush of water drowning all other sounds. Fifty metres away, the grizzly closed on it, covering the ground in great, leaping bounds.

The caribou tossed water over its neck and shoulders, then shook itself. Lazily, it turned its head and stared in disbelief for a long, wasted moment. The bear started to roar at the top of its voice. The caribou leapt sideways in shock, its hooves sliding on the weed-covered bed of the stream. Frantically, it struggled to keep its balance.

The grizzly reared up on his hind legs, flinging his arms around the caribou's neck. They fell together with a tremendous crash, the caribou bellowing with terror as they rolled over and over in the water. The caribou lashed out. One of his knees driving up into the bear's ribs with bone-cracking force. The grizzly grunted in pain. And for a second relaxed his grip.

The caribou came lurching up the bank, kicking and bucking, desperate to get clear. The grizzly swiped at its underbelly, his claws slicing through the hide. The caribou screamed. Then it had reached the top of the bank and was running for its life. Its head thrown back, its eyes rolling in terror.

But the caribou was badly hurt. Marak saw that at once. It was stumbling and the smell of blood was suddenly everywhere. Behind it, the grizzly followed at a shambling run. The bear caught up and for the next ten metres kept pace with the bull. The grizzly drew back a paw and slapped the caribou across the muzzle.

The caribou veered away, lashing out with its back legs and missing. Seconds later the bear was alongside again. Another blow. The caribou screamed. And another. Maddened with pain, the caribou twisted round, put its antlers down and charged. The bear reared up on his hind legs, three metres tall, his long claws waiting. The caribou's head thudded into his stomach, lifting the bear clear of the ground.

The grizzly fell forward between the spread of antlers hugging the caribou around the neck again. The caribou snorted in triumph and tried to throw the bear over his back. But the grizzly hung on. His powerful arms tightening in a vice-like grip. His massive weight pivoting across the caribou's shoulders.

For five minutes they stayed locked together, straining for advantage. The heat from their bodies rising into the midnight sky. And then at last, one of the caribou's front legs began to shake. It buckled. The caribou went down on one knee with a long moan of despair.

The bear leant further over, balancing now on the caribou's neck. The other knee gave way and the caribou fell to the ground. It waited with its head outstretched. Too exhausted to move. The grizzly raised a massive fist and brought it down with a heavy thud across the back of the caribou's neck. There was a crack. The caribou pitched forward. Its legs thrashed for a moment as it made one final, desperate attempt to get up. Then it collapsed and lay still. The grizzly roared in triumph and dragged it over on its side. Then it shuffled round towards the stomach.

Keeping a respectful distance, Marak circled the grizzly. It was a futile gesture but it made him feel better. The bear roared, warning him off. But when it realized Marak was on his own, the bear ignored him. The sound of the grizzly eating tortured Marak. When he couldn't stand it any longer he turned and ran. The soft squelches and lip-smackings followed him for a very long way.

He ran on blindly, conscious only of the longing

to eat. He ran through woods and swam across a lake, now clear of melting ice. He spotted a beaver lodge not far from the shore and swam towards it. When he got closer, he stopped paddling and drifted silently down towards it until the lodge towered over him.

The beavers had young ones in there. He listened to their mewings and squeaks and heard the chuckles and grunts of the parents as they fussed over their kittens. Marak trod water, waiting patiently in case either of the adults left the lodge. But they must have heard him because it became very still. He headed for the shore. There was no point waiting any longer.

He splashed through the shallows and ran up a steep hillside. When he reached the top, he stopped and put his head back. A long mournful cry slowly welled up inside him. It echoed across the hills and forests, swamps and lakes. A sad, inconsolable story. Marak's voice deepened. He howled in misery. He howled his hunger. He howled for Claw and his pack. Lastly, he howled his own dreadful loneliness.

The sky was clear and full of stars. They stretched over his head like some huge canopy of twinkling ice. He stared at them uncomprehendingly. And then, from somewhere far over the horizon, he heard an answering chorus of howls!

Twenty-seven

Marak was electrified. He sprang to his feet barking in delight. New energy sparkled through his entire body. He was no longer on his own! For the last month he had neither met nor found a trace of any other wolf. For the very first time in his life he had been totally alone.

He howled again, this time in pure delight. All the loneliness and misery of the last month forgotten in the joy of the moment. He strained his ears and thought he heard an answering cry. But couldn't be sure. He listened patiently while the gentle, pre-dawn breeze sprang up and began fingering the tops of the trees.

The pack must be on the move and now out of range. He looked at the rapidly brightening sky and mentally fixed the direction the howling had come from. Then he set off at a run to find them.

The going became harder as he went further north. There was deep slush everywhere. He did find a careless squirrel digging up a cache of nuts, and downed it in two quick gulps. Much later, he heard the sound of a small waterfall. He trotted past, studying it intently. There was something about the shape of the rocks and the narrow ravine at its foot.

Excitement began building inside him. He picked his way along the top of the ravine. Below him, the water boiled between vertical slabs of rock. A fine mist hung over everything. He pushed through a dense screen of ferns. And there in front of him was an old familiar cottonwood tree lying on its side, bright green with moss. He whined in pleasure.

It was his tree! He had used it as a scenting post. It marked the boundary between his territory and that of his neighbour, Yellow Nose. He ran towards it barking in excitement. He was home!

But as he got nearer, his pace slackened. Something was wrong. He listened but could hear nothing above the roar of the water. Slowly, he padded forward to investigate. The ground was churned up all round the tree. The snow heavily stained.

He found Yellow Nose's scent immediately. Yellow Nose was old for a wolf in the wild. He was nearly ten and had led his pack for the last six winters. Marak decided they had been here two, perhaps three days ago. Six of them. So Yellow Nose had also had a bad winter. Last autumn, he remembered, there had been a dozen in his pack.

But there were other markings. Scents Marak did not recognize. Very fresh. Made only a few hours ago. Bitter-smelling warnings splashed liberally along the dead tree and on the surrounding bushes. Strangers. A new pack. And very aggressive. Warning Yellow Nose to keep away. Threatening to take over his territory. And claiming what had been Marak's!

A deep growl rose in the wolf's chest. It had never occurred to him that another pack would move in and take over his territory. He had lived here all his life. This was his hunting ground. He had won it when he had fought for leadership. It was his by right. He would fight to get it back. Angrily, he called for Claw, then remembered she was gone.

Some sixth sense made him look back along the

way he had come. He thought he saw a fern leaf shiver. Why should a fern move on a morning when there was no wind? Then it was still again. He stared at it. And decided it was a mouse or a shrew scurrying between the stalks. Preoccupied, he forgot about it.

A crow cawed and flew in front of him. It landed heavily in the branches of a birch tree and began scolding. Marak ignored it. He left his own mark along the dead cottonwood. Then after a moment's hesitation, he began to push his way through the undergrowth.

It had always been gloomy in this part of the forest. Even at the height of summer, the sun rarely penetrated the tree tops. Generations of trees lay where they had fallen, some still almost upright. And all of them gently rotting. The air smelt dank. Marak shivered and felt strangely vulnerable. He heard the sharp cry of an animal in pain and a series of loud grunts. A wolverine was feeding nearby.

He licked his lips and ran to investigate. There was a sudden rush in front of him. A white-tailed deer bolted, less than ten metres away. It had been standing motionless in a clump of alders, watching the wolf approach. Then its nerve broke.

Marak was after it in a flash, knowing the deer was at a disadvantage. The trees were too close together. The deer was leaping and dodging between them, desperate to find a clear run. The underbrush snatched at its legs. And all the time, it knew the wolf was closing the gap. Marak could smell its panic, the sharp smell of ammonia that was already clinging to its sides.

Then through the trees, he saw a gleam of sunlight and remembered the bare hillside where the trees had all died. The deer saw it too, hesitated, and tried to twist round in mid-stride. It landed badly, slipping and colliding with the trunk of a tree. It leapt to its feet but by then it was far too late. Marak sprang high over its back and brought it down in one easy, fluid movement. By the time they crashed to the ground, Marak's teeth had already found their mark.

He ate greedily, swallowing the meat in chunks, driven on by a growing sense of unease. Twice he raised his head and snarled into the gloom. When he had eaten as much as he could, he walked to the edge of the trees and lay down. Behind him, the crow flew down and landed clumsily beside the kill.

The forest was very quiet. Only the insects seemed busy. Marak's concentration began to wander. He was trying to remember a hide he had once found. A cave high up in the rocks. And not very far from here. He could picture the actual entrance quite clearly. It would make a good place to watch from until he knew more about these intruders.

Sixty metres ahead, a whitethroat flew out of a bush, complaining loudly. Marak yawned. He couldn't help it. The sun was hot and he was gorged with meat. He shook his head and tried to keep awake. He had to find this safe hiding place. By tonight.

Not far away, a claw scraped against a stone. He looked around, not sure what he had heard. Then everything went suddenly very still. Marak's hackles began to rise. He scrambled up. And watched in disbelief. Like grey ghosts, the pack broke cover and moved menacingly towards him.

Twenty-eight

Mel was in a filthy mood. Nothing was going right.
Two of the ranch hands had taken a vehicle the
night before and crashed it. Worse still, he had a
feeling that Mr Daniels blamed him for the wolf's
escape. Nothing had been said. Just the odd heavy
look and sarcastic remark.

He left the ranch office moodily. Those damn
Viccarys! he thought, closing the door behind him
with a bang. Everyone knew they had let the wolf
go. What was there to prove? And that silly old guy,
Price. He should have sacked both of them, and had
done with it.

Mel cursed silently and kicked at a pine cone. It
hit one of the dustbins outside the cookhouse and
spun away. O'Shaugnessy, the cook, came out on to

the top step. He was carrying a box full of empty tins. He saw Mel and grinned. 'Hi there, Mel!' he called cheerily. 'Look like you've lost a dollar and found a penny.'

Mel said nothing. He wasn't in the business of being friendly with people like O'Shaugnessy. He watched the man drag an empty bin away from the stack and begin dumping tins inside it.

'Is there any news of your wolf?' O'Shaugnessy called out. 'I bet you'll be missing him something terrible!' And he laughed.

Mel's fists clenched. He strode towards the cook, his face working with anger. O'Shaugnessy dropped the bin and began to back away, his hands fluttering in apology. Then he leapt for the steps and bolted up them just ahead of Mel's kick. The door banged behind him and the key turned in the lock.

Mel rattled the handle and pounded on the door. 'You little jerk!' he shouted. 'I'll break your neck next time I see you!' Seething with rage, he turned away. The dustbin lay on its side surrounded by empty tins. Flies were already crawling over them.

Something caught his eye. It was lying in the dust where the bin had stood. Ordinarily, he would have ignored it, but today was different. Something inside him insisted he go and take a look. Perhaps it belonged to O'Shaugnessy. He might have lost it and be looking for it. Well, he sure as heck wouldn't find it now.

He stooped down and pulled out an old baseball cap. He recognized the logo on the front. 'New York Yankees,' he muttered to himself. Then frowned, wondering who supported 'The Yankees' out here. He couldn't think of anyone. He tried it on. It was too small. He turned the cap over. Someone's initials were neatly printed on the inside rim. No one he knew.

He stared at the cap, puzzling about it. It was all wrong. Out of place. So what was it doing here? He got to his feet and looked round. This was where the cage had been. He tried to put the cap on again . . . and began to smile. 'Gotcha!' he breathed. The next moment, he was running as if his life depended on it, his face flushed with triumph.

Twenty-nine

There were ten of them. Marak remained motionless. He saw the yearlings circling round behind him but ignored them. His eyes fixed on the two wolves slowly approaching him.

They stopped five metres away. Black Fang, the pack leader, was a head smaller than Marak. An old wolf with a scarred nose and face. He had deep-set eyes and uneven teeth. He walked stiff-legged towards Marak, the fur bristling along his back and sides until he looked almost twice his normal size. He stared unblinkingly at Marak, challenging him to back down. Then he drew back his lips in a ferocious snarl. His mate stopped and waited. Marak saw she was heavily in cub.

Marak watched him coming and hatred rose inside

him. This was the animal who had invaded his territory. This was the upstart who now hunted over his land. Whose mate was about to strengthen his pack still further. Marak's eyes never left his face, staring the intruder down. Demanding Black Fang's total submission.

But even as his rage grew, Marak's mind raced, assessing his own chances of survival. It was too late to turn tail and flee. He might just have got away had he fled immediately. But not now. Not when he was openly challenging Black Fang like this.

Even if Marak submitted and rolled over on his back, Black Fang would still kill him. Marak was too big a threat to him and his pack. There was only one thing to do. He must incapacitate Black Fang somehow and then run for his life in the subsequent confusion. Killing him would only provoke his mate and the rest of the pack into a mad bloodlust.

Black Fang was very close now. Only two body lengths separated them. Stiffly, they circled each other. The watching pack started to bark and moan. Marak saw the gleam in Black Fang's eyes. The next instant, the old wolf sprang for his throat.

Marak spun away, his shoulder blocking the attack. Black Fang slashed at it. Blood spurted all along the wound. Marak gasped in pain. The old wolf crouched, his tail lashing the ground. Then he launched himself at Marak. They met head on.

They wrestled, chest to chest. Long claws ripping at the other's head and sides. Fangs locked, jaws grinding together. Razor sharp teeth biting at the bloody froth along the other's muzzle. Hate-filled eyes barely centimetres apart, fighting for advantage.

Gradually, Marak's size and weight began to force the other down. Black Fang took a step backwards and then another. His mate screamed at him. Marak felt him start to tremble violently. The next instant he had gone limp, slipping through Marak's hold. Before Marak could stop him, Black Fang was ducking under him and tearing at his stomach.

The pack howled. Black Fang corkscrewed to one side and leapt away, still untouched. Now he began mocking Marak, yapping at him like a puppy. Twice Marak ran at him. Both times Black Fang sprang clear, unscathed. But his teeth raked Marak's shoulders. Blood was running freely down Marak's chest and legs. He was panting hard, sucking down air.

He charged Black Fang a third time, his head

deliberately held higher, exposing his neck. Black Fang saw his chance. And took it! He sprang at Marak, his eyes blazing in triumph. His jaws gaped wide for the killer bite and snapped shut – at empty air. Marak was already twisting under his great leap. His teeth closed over Black Fang's outstretched leg and bit down with bone-cracking force.

Black Fang screamed and pitched head over heels. He hit the ground heavily and rolled over and over. His mate jumped away from him in panic. The pack milled around, uncertain what to do, howling loudly. Marak did not wait a moment longer.

He was off, running as hard as he could, knowing he had to get back into Yellow Nose's territory to be remotely safe. Black Fang would come after him as soon as he got back on his feet. Already, two fully-grown yearlings had realized what was happening and were racing in to cut him off.

Marak flattened his ears against his skull and turned to meet them. He hit the nearest one with his shoulder, tumbling him over in a confusion of legs and bloody jaws. As he strode clear, the second wolf was on him, biting at Marak's flank and injured shoulder.

Marak spun round, slipped and fell on top of

him. The yearling panicked, tried to pull himself clear but by then, Marak had him by the throat. A quick, deep bite and Marak was up and running. He snatched a look backwards. Black Fang was on his feet, lurching awkwardly. He was whimpering in pain. Marak could also hear the frightened cries of the two yearlings. And Black Fang's mate urging the others to chase and kill him.

It was not difficult to follow Marak's trail. He was bleeding from a dozen wounds. The pack pursued him for a couple of kilometres, but only in a half-hearted way. Marak knew they were content to see him off their territory. They gave up the chase at the edge of a lake.

He waded out and sank gratefully into the water. He swam slowly, knowing the pack wouldn't follow. When he reached the far side, he shook himself like a dog and began to lick his wounds. The cold lake water had stopped most of the bleeding. But now a reaction was setting in.

His body was battered and beginning to ache painfully. The flesh around the bites and scratch marks was already swollen. His head drooped and he began to shake with exhaustion. But he still had to find a safe place to hide. He was in another pack's territory. And he knew if they found him like this, there would be no escape.

He walked for a mile then, exhausted, curled up beside a fallen tree and fell into a deep sleep. But not for long. One moment he was dead to the world. The next, his eyes were wide open. There was another animal nearby, a large animal. He was sure of it. And where there was one, there could be many more.

He strained his ears to listen. There was a long silence. He was stiff and cold and convinced he had heard something. His nose was clogged with dried blood. It might just be a clumsy black bear. Or a grizzly . . .

A foot brushed against some of last year's dead pine needles. And then paused. Marak swallowed. Whatever it was, it knew he was there. Lying behind this dead tree. He held his breath. There it was again! Getting closer. Dangerously close!

He sprang to his feet, eyes gleaming with menace and with fight. His snarls died in his throat. He stared in disbelief. For a long time. A young, solitary, female wolf stood poised for flight immediately in front of him.

Thirty

Her name was Ootak. She was three years old and had been driven from her pack by a jealous, dominant female. She attacked Ootak without warning, refusing to let her feed with the rest of them. In the end, Ootak stole away.

She was silvery grey in colour, with white undersides. Marak stared at the bite marks on her ears and nose and saw the raggedness of her tail. He wagged his tail in growing delight. She was a solitary like him.

She dropped down in front of him and began to whimper. Slowly, she dragged herself towards him in submission, her eyes fixed on his face. Marak jumped over the tree trunk and stood beside her. She raised her head and licked his jaws.

She ran her tongue gently along the torn edges of his mouth, comforting him with little growls and whines. She cleaned away the blood and dirt from his shoulder. And Marak let her. He stood perfectly still while she did so, his eyes closed. Delighting in the rare sense of well-being that was growing within him.

When she had finished, they touched noses. Marak's tail wagged. Immediately, Ootak crouched, arching her back like a puppy. He bent towards her. She licked his nose. Marak dropped down in front of her, his eyes bright with excitement. He put his head between his paws and stared at her.

She growled at him and flicked her tail. Marak snarled and shot out a paw. She jumped back a few centimetres, daring him to do it again. Marak feinted with his other paw. Ootak barked at him, short, high-pitched cries, and half stood up. Marak's jaws opened in a huge grin. He sprang towards her.

But Ootak was up in a flash, darting away from him. Marak gave a yip and chased after her. Ootak ran like the wind, dodging behind trees, doubling back on herself, encouraging Marak to catch her, then twisting away at the last moment.

She was nimbler than him and impossible to wrong-foot.

They raced along the lakeshore, their feet kicking up a long line of splashes. A pair of ducks flew off, quacking indignantly, the downbeat from their wings furrowing the black stillness of the water.

Ootak slipped round a pile of rocks, then quickly scrambled upwards. She waited until Marak was underneath then leapt down on top of him. The two of them rolled over and over, growling ferociously and beating at each other with their paws.

Marak tired first. He flopped down on a bank of shingle, his tongue lolling. She let him sleep for half an hour keeping watch throughout, then woke him. He followed her to the safe place she had found at the foot of a low cliff. It was a perfect hiding place. The entrance was screened by bushes. It was very narrow and Marak had to squeeze and shrug his way in.

Inside, the floor was sandy and dry. Marak's shoulder was aching and painful. Fresh blood dripped down on to his fur. Ootak watched while he cleaned himself. After he had fallen asleep, she waited just inside the entrance, listening and watching. It began to rain. Satisfied, she went and lay down beside Marak, happier now than she could ever remember. They slept back to back like dogs, content.

Thirty-one

The days passed in a warm glow of happiness. They ran and played together, fighting mock battles over pine cones. They swam in the lake and tried catching the speckled trout that lay motionless in the shallows. But no matter how carefully they crept up on them, the fish were as elusive as quicksilver.

They found an old male skunk and teased him unmercifully, leaping over him and dodging out of the way in the nick of time. When the smell became too rank, they ran to a different part of the forest. And all the time, Marak's love of his beautiful mate grew.

When finally hunger dragged them back to reality, they quickly learnt how to hunt together. In the weeks that followed, they perfected their skills. Marak would trot off to one side for several hundred metres, then circle back. Ootak would wait until she judged he was somewhere in front of her, then walk casually towards him.

Early that morning she flushed out a plump young deer. She gave chase, alerting Marak with a series of sharp barks. Anticipating their progress, he quickly closed on them. The deer had a brief glimpse of the wolf running towards it, before it was catapulted to the ground with bone-splintering force. Ootak and Marak ate it where it had fallen. When they had finished, a delightful lassitude stole over both of them. Soon, they fell asleep . . .

Now, Ootak opened one eye. Five metres away, a huge raven stood watching her, its head on one side. It saw her move and gave a scream of rage. It rushed at her, its wings half open, the feathers stiff and bristling. The thick, stabbing beak hurling abuse.

She sat up. The raven stopped in its tracks and hopped sideways, screaming shrilly. Ootak looked round, puzzled by its behaviour. Marak lay fast asleep on the other side of the carcass. She looked at him and saw his full stomach. Her eyes softened.

The raven took off with much beating of wings. She watched it fly up into the branches of a tree and suddenly realized that the air was thick with birds. There were crows and other ravens impatiently circling overhead. She could see them staring down at her. Even further above, a pair of buzzards hung motionless against the blue sky.

She sprang to her feet and stared at the sun. It was noticeably lower. Mid-afternoon. They had slept for hours! Her bark brought Marak to his feet with a snarl. One look at the sky told him the worst. Every predator for miles would have seen that swirling flock of birds and would know exactly what it meant. Including the pack whose territory this was!

He barked at her in fury, biting at her jaws, growling and snarling. Savage with fear and his own stupidity. He had broken one of the basic rules of survival. There was never any mercy for poachers. Then he was off, running for his life. All his senses stretched to outwit or outrun whatever form the danger took. There could be only one warning. After that it would be too late. Ootak followed close behind, blood glistening on her jaw.

Thirty-two

They were being followed. Silently, remorselessly, the pack was after them. A strong, powerful pack which had found the deer he and Ootak had eaten earlier. An hour ago, the pack had begun howling. Marak and Ootak had stopped to listen, shifting uneasily as they listened to the rage. And the threats. Then the howling stopped.

Ootak had made a show of grooming herself to hide her fear. Marak listened impassively, gauging the strength of the pack and its closeness. There were at least twelve of them. And now they were closing in. Marak imagined them running swiftly between the trees, keeping out of sight until the last moment, to maintain surprise.

He looked over his shoulder. And looked again,

convinced he could see a darker shape in the shadows. He shook his head, furious with himself. He was seeing things. Growing jittery at a time when their survival demanded he keep all his wits about him.

The air was warm and the night full of movement. Marak's ears flicked ceaselessly. Listening for the sounds of pursuit. A branch springing back into place. A powerful body brushing past a tree. The urgent pad of running feet. That moment was coming, he was sure of it.

He looked across at Ootak. She was running strongly. Only the flecks of foam along her mouth showed how desperate the situation was. The pack would kill her first. They both knew that. They would get in between them and force her away from his side. They would take as long as they wanted before dragging her down and ripping out her throat. They would do this to prolong his own terror. To show him who was the stronger. It was Nature.

There was a new sound. A dull booming noise. Somewhere in front of him. He tried to ignore it but it grew louder and more insistent, forcing him to listen. It was a strange sound. There was strength there and power. And something else. A warning.

He stumbled as he realized what it was.

A river. A big one, tumbling between rocky sides. He came to a skidding halt, his feet furrowing the ground. Which way to go? He hesitated, looked at Ootak and was off, running hard and keeping the roar of the river to his left. Great slabs of rock began to appear, pushing up through the ground. The trees thinned then shrank away. There was a fine spray of mist in the air. He turned away from it, heading back towards the trees.

And saw the wolf! It was standing beside a low bush some way ahead of them. It saw Marak at the same time and put its head back and howled. A short, urgent cry audible even above the rumble of the water. Beyond it, another wolf ran out. Marak heard Ootak barking and looked back. Then he stopped, knowing it was the end. He turned and faced the rest of them.

Forty metres away, he saw the gleam of long white teeth and smelt the frenzy of the pack. Their heads went back in a howl of exaltation. They milled round, snarling and barking, urging each other on. He watched them come running in and felt helpless. They seemed to move quite slowly and he was surprised by that.

Ootak was screaming at him. He looked at her, not understanding. Her teeth slashed at his nose and the sudden pain shocked him to his senses. She raced away, ears flat against her skull. He chased after her. All round them, the rocks dripped with moisture. His feet slipped and for an instant he slid sideways. He snatched a look behind. Ten more strides and the pack would be on him. There was no escape.

There was a large clump of bracken in front. For some reason he wanted to reach it. Ootak had disappeared. He didn't know where. But it was too late to worry. The howling was all around him. Teeth snatched at his tail. He gathered himself and leapt over the bracken. And saw the boiling surface of the river far below him.

The river held Marak deep in its ice-cold depths. It tumbled him head over tail in a bewildering, roller coaster of a ride. Feebly, he pawed at the smooth green wave that swooped and raced and sent him spinning round the sides of great boulders.

He was in a nightmare world of crashing stones, sucking whirlpools and pounding waves. His head was full of exploding lights. His lungs bursting. A current seized his legs and shot him to the surface.

He gulped at the night air. A wave slapped him in the face and he choked. There was no time to recover. The river plucked him under, tail first, whirling him off on his back. He tried to turn on to his side, but the current held him in a vice-like grip. Sometimes his head broke the surface and he snatched a breath of spray-filled air. He had brief glimpses of the stars jerking crazily above him. Then the river would roar over him again and drag him under.

As his lungs filled with water, the terrible pain in his chest began to ease. After a while, he no longer bothered to struggle. He was aware of the river all around him, of jagged rocks towering out of the spray and waves bursting against them. But he was feeling more and more detached from it all.

He remembered the pack and their howls of frustration. They had a good territory. They were right to drive him out. He would have done the same. He thought about Ootak and remembered her scent. He felt very tired and began to drift in and out of consciousness.

Much later, he realized the river was quieter. There were no waves. It was flowing steadily and he could feel the current pushing him forwards. It was a soothing motion. His head was out of the water, breathing was easy. He began to look around.

It was light. Not long after dawn. The river was much wider here and flowing between low banks. He noticed a clump of trees a hundred metres ahead of him and started paddling towards them. He could lie up there and sleep. There might even be food nearby.

The current was strengthening. Alarmed, he dug deep with his paws and tried to angle his body in towards the shore. But the trees were already gliding past. And then he heard it! A far-off thunder that made him yelp in despair. He knew that sound.

His paws tore at the water. His head went up in panic. The river was accelerating all around him. He was imprisoned in a long glass wave which swept him over the falls like a bundle of rags. For a moment, he hung clear in mid-air, looking down into the thunder. Then he was dropping like a stone into the middle of it.

Thirty-three

Life was a long time returning. For hours, Marak inhabited a grey, shadowy world where nothing was real. Dimly, he became aware that he was lying on a wide bank of pebbles at the water's edge, with no clear memory of ever getting there.

Every bone in his body felt broken. Breathing hurt. He tried to sit up and fell back moaning in pain. The sun was shining. It was hot on his face. Mosquitoes were dancing in front of his nose. But he was alive!

He staggered upright and stood bemused as water gushed from his nostrils and mouth. He retched loudly, staring at the ground, barely comprehending, and saw a shadow join his. Ootak stood beside him, encouraging him with loud whimpers of affection and relief. She licked his face and ears, crooning to him.

He took a step forwards and waited until the cramp faded. Gingerly, he took another and another. He sneezed violently and brought up more water. And felt better. He tried trotting up and down, then stood growling while the blood returned. Soon, the muscles in his legs and shoulders began to ease.

She lay down beside him, silently communicating. Being lighter than Marak, the river had tossed her aside much sooner. She had been caught in a backwash, eventually drifting down into a mass of old tree branches and other flotsam, close to the shore. At first, she had waited for Marak, then slowly, had made her way downstream, searching for him.

She had stood at the top of the falls for a long time, watching the river hurl itself to destruction. She had listened to the thunder and heard other voices there urging her to jump. When she finally spotted his body lying half in, half out of the water a mile below the falls, she ran forward more in grief than with any expectation of life.

But he *was* alive. Just! She seized him by the scruff of the neck and tried to drag him clear. But she lacked the strength to move him. For almost an hour, she had stood over him, barking at him, nipping his ear and nose, trying to wake him. She fell asleep on her feet and collapsed, unable to do more.

Marak butted her gently and growled. She snarled at him in mock anger and bit his lower jaw. They tussled like yearlings, standing upright and boxing each other's head and chest. Marak's huge jaws seized her by the neck. Then he licked her affectionately and shook himself. He puffed out his fur and started cleaning his front.

He thought of food and was immediately hungry. He gave a huge yawn, stretched to his full length, and ran at a gentle lope towards the nearby forest. He stopped just inside the first line of trees. Ootak saw his body droop and ran towards him.

The scents were fresh. Made by yet another pack and less than a day old. Their message was hostile and brief. Marak's great head turned towards Ootak in despair. The pack would be somewhere close. Hunting this part of their territory.

Marak stared at the river. They were trapped again. A blind rage seized him. Nature had not fashioned him to be a solitary animal. To be always running away like this. Forever crossing other wolves' territory. Looking over his shoulder and into the shadows.

He was an alpha male. It was his right to have his own pack. With Ootak as his mate. Her loyalty to him was absolute. He knew that. So it was up to him. He must stake out a territory for both of them. But where?

A faint memory began to stir somewhere at the back of his mind. He remembered the moose herd. Hundreds and hundreds of them. And humans and the cage. He shivered and looked round quickly at the silent depths of the forest. But there were also woods where he had run for days and never seen or heard a human or another wolf. Unclaimed territory. Yes! He remembered now.

He stepped back into the sunshine. Ootak was staring at him. Puzzled. He looked at the sky and knew which direction he must follow. She barked, questioning him. Knowing he had decided. His tail began to wag.

They ran in and out of the shallows to avoid leaving a trail. Later during the night, they would have to begin cutting through the mountains. And when that was over, they must cross the badlands. But that was many days ahead of them. He looked round at Ootak. And growled happily.

Thirty-four

Amy read the invitation for a second time. There was no mistake. 'You're not going to believe this,' she told her husband. 'It's from Mary-Jane Daniels. They want us to come to their barbecue next weekend.' She looked at the card again. 'To welcome in the summer,' she read.

'They have one every year,' Jessica informed them. 'It's the big event round here. Everyone goes.'

'How do you know?' Ed challenged.

'My friends have been talking about it for days,' she told him simply.

Rick looked at his wife. 'Should we go to it?'

She made a face. 'They're the only people who've asked us to anything lately.' She thought a little more. 'Heck! Why not? Perhaps we're back in favour again.'

'Hope you're right,' said Rick.

'Well, it'll be fun for the kids,' Amy smiled.

The following Saturday evening, the Viccarys joined a long tailback of vehicles and parked their car in a field close to the Daniels' ranch. Although the shadows were lengthening, it was still pleasantly warm.

'You were right,' Rick told Jessica.

'Looks like the whole town's here,' Amy agreed.

'When does it finish?' asked Ed gloomily.

'At midnight. After the dancing,' Jessica enthused.

'Oh Ed! Come on now,' his mother chided. 'You'll enjoy it. It was very nice of Mrs Daniels to ask us.'

Ed shrugged. 'Well, don't say I didn't warn you.'

'They're roasting an ox,' Jessica added. 'And there's a live group.'

'It's a Country and Western band,' Ed reminded them. 'Yuk!'

But by the time the moon appeared, the Viccarys were quite enjoying themselves. Daniels, wearing a tall chef's hat, was full of cheerful laughter as he turned steaks and sausages and chickens on a huge, outdoor barbecue. Behind him, the ox roasted over a spitting fire. Charcoal glowed red, beer and coke cans hissed open and the conversation levels went steadily up.

The Viccarys were watching the band when a large figure loomed up beside them. 'Glad to see you like good music!' said Sheriff Hoskins. 'No hard feelings, eh?'

Rick stuck out his hand. 'None at all, sheriff. None at all.' Then added, quietly, 'Thanks for dropping the charges!'

After he had gone, Amy looked at Rick and grinned. 'Local elections must be coming up!'

A little later, Ed made an excuse and went off on his own. There was something he had to do. Something he had been secretly planning ever since the invitation had arrived. He slipped between the rows of outbuildings, leaving the sounds of the party behind. He stopped at the cookhouse, his eyes searching for the place where the cage had been. He took a deep breath and knelt down. This was where the wolf had stood staring at him. Where it had licked him. It was a wonderful feeling.

Somebody coughed. 'Lost something!' said Mel, coming out of the shadows. An icy hand brushed Ed's spine. His mouth went dry. He started to back away. Mel followed, his face chalk white in the moonlight.

There was a distant shout of laughter and the band struck up. Ed's shoulders touched the side of the building behind. Mel's shadow loomed over him. 'Been waiting for you,' he hissed and his hand shot out, reaching for the boy's hair. Ed twisted under it and ran. Mel grinned and spat. It was time to rejoin the party.

Rick Viccary nudged his wife. The moment he had been dreading was rapidly approaching. Daniels was walking towards them. He had taken off his cook's hat and was wearing his usual stetson. He carried a beer in one hand.

He raised his hat to Amy and smiled at them. 'Hope you folks are enjoying yourselves?'

'Yes! Great!' Rick told him, summoning up a polite smile. He put his arm around Amy. 'Good party. Thanks for inviting us.'

Daniels' smile broadened. 'Glad you could come. I was hoping you would. We've got something to show you.'

He put his hands on his hips and looked round. 'Hey! Everybody!' he shouted. 'Come on over here a minute!'

Amy frowned but, before she could say anything, Ed pushed in beside her, looking flustered. He was out of breath. Daniels was shouting again and that distracted her. The crowd round them was growing rapidly.

Ed looked up and saw Mel approaching. Their eyes met. Ed shivered and quickly looked away. Daniels held up his arms for quiet. 'I've got an apology to make!' he called.

Everyone stared at him with interest. Ed saw Mr Price in the crowd. He was looking puzzled. Near him, Pete Daniels was standing, holding a plastic supermarket bag. The rancher cleared his throat and continued.

'A month or so ago,' he began, 'I was convinced that either Rick Viccary or even Amy, had come up here at night . . . and broken in . . . and set free that wolf. The one we all know about.'

He had their complete attention now. 'Anyone seen the sheriff?' he shouted, looking over their heads.

'Rick!' Amy hissed, digging her fingers into his arm. 'What's happening!'

There was a burst of chatter as Sheriff Hoskins pushed his way through. The rancher greeted him with a warm handshake. 'This wolf,' Daniels continued, 'was the biggest thing I ever saw. It was huge. Right, sheriff?'

The crowd craned their necks. 'He was a monster!' Hoskins agreed.

'It was on television,' someone shouted. And there was an excited hum of recall.

Amy's hand gripped Rick's.

Daniels raised his arms again for silence and gazed round. 'So, let me tell you folks, why I was wrong to blame Rick or Amy. Why I was wrong to think either of them would come out here in the dead of night to let that wolf go.' He swung round. 'Pete! Bring that bag here!'

He dipped his hand inside. 'Because of this!' he shouted in a hoarse voice. 'We found it right beside the place we kept the wolf.' He paused dramatically then held up a baseball cap. 'New York Yankees! Anyone round here support them?'

Ed's skin crawled.

A couple of men catcalled. Everyone else looked puzzled.

'Now, how do you suppose this thing got here? And who dropped it?' The rancher's voice became conversational. 'Well now, let's make it easy for everyone.' He examined the cap in an elaborate pantomine, then he smiled round at his guests. 'I do believe the owner's initials are here inside.'

Jessica stared at her brother.

'E.V.' Daniels announced. 'And it's a boy's! Too small for an adult! See here!' And he rammed the cap down on Pete's head.

'Ed?' gasped Amy.

Rick's arm was round his son's shoulders, holding him tightly. It took the crowd a few more seconds to make the connection. They gasped.

Daniels looked round in triumph. 'It's Ed Viccary's!' he jeered. 'They sent a kid to do a man's work!'

Something snapped inside Ed. He could hear himself yelling. He threw off Rick's hand and struggled through the crowd, barging into people, knocking hot dogs and slices of pizza out of their hands. His father was shouting. Struggling after him.

Then he was out in front of everyone. On his own. Confronting the hard-faced rancher and his son. Hating them with every fragment of his being.

'I did it!' he bawled. 'I did it on my own! My folks know nothing!' He glared round at the crowd. Their faces were a blur. 'And I'd do it again! Any time!'

There was a stunned silence. The crowd gaped. No one moved. Then, from far away, a long, mournful cry broke the stillness. They listened, transfixed. Shivering suddenly in the warm night air. As the crescendo died away, another voice took its place. A lighter, gentler one.

Daniels' eyes bulged. He hurled the cap at the boy. 'They're back!' he raged. 'Damn you, Ed Viccary! Damn the lot of you!'

Thirty-five

'Ed! I'm so proud of you!' Rick called over his shoulder. 'So proud! You're a brave guy! Did you really let the wolf go?' The car hit a pothole, jerking them out of their seats. Rick shouted an apology and grabbed at the steering wheel.

Jessica laughed in excitement. 'He sure did! He told me eveything! Did you see Pete Daniels' face?'

Amy reached for his hand. 'Ed! It's wonderful. You did fantastically well! But why didn't you tell us before? You could have been hurt!'

'Or caught!' Rick put in, soberly. 'Be home in ten minutes.'

'Wasn't it weird when the wolves began to howl?' Jessica cried. 'Like they knew what was going on. Do you think they did?'

Ed said nothing. He put his head back on the seat and closed his eyes. The wolf had come back. The same wolf. He was sure of it. What on earth would happen now?

Later, they sat round the kitchen table while he told them what had happened. 'I'm really sorry about the baseball cap,' he said at the end. 'That's messed up everything.'

Rick spread his hands. 'I expect old man Price will suspend us or something. But let's keep things in perspective.' He shrugged. 'You did the right thing! I wish I'd had the guts!' And he rumpled Ed's hair.

'That goes for me too!' Amy came round and hugged him. Then she hugged Jessica.

'OK! OK!' Rick said gruffly, his voice not quite under control. 'Can we back up a little and see where we're at?' He looked at Ed. 'My guess is that your wolf has found himself a mate.'

'So that's a breeding pair,' Amy nodded, looking very pleased.

'Now we can call the folks at Yellowstone,' Jessica cried. 'And they'll come and pick them up!'

'We've got to find them first,' Ed reminded her. 'That's not going to be easy.'

'There's hundreds of square miles out there, honey,' said Amy, touching her hand. 'They could be anywhere.'

Jessica's face fell.

'It's even worse than that,' said Rick, quietly. 'Everyone's going to get involved. All the cattlemen for a start. They'll have trucks and ranch hands on horses. And don't forget, Daniels has got a helicopter. Then there's the sheriff and all the patrol cars. They're going to move heaven and earth to get to them first.'

'And kill them,' Jessica sniffed, suddenly close to tears.

'They'll use radios and e-mails to coordinate things,' Ed added gloomily.

'And there's only four of us,' Amy reminded them. They stared at her and silently agreed. It sounded hopeless.

Rick shook his head. 'They'll be putting out poisoned bait as well.' He glanced at his wife. 'What do they use these days? Strychnine?'

She nodded. 'It burns out their stomachs and it's cheap.'

Ed puffed out his cheeks. 'We need a miracle,' he breathed.

The telephone rang. Rick got up. 'Wonder which well-wisher this is going to be!' It was Mr Price. Rick rolled his eyes and leaned against the sink. He looked at Amy and began to relay the conversation. '. . . And you'd like us not to come in for the next week or two . . . let the dust settle . . . OK, Mr Price . . . I understand! Bye for now!'

As he replaced the receiver, it rang again. 'Yes!' Then his expression changed. 'It's for you, Ed. Your friend, Jimmy Skagawa.'

Ed listened in silence. He put down the phone and looked puzzled. 'He says his grandad wants to talk to me. Says he's got something pretty important to tell us about the wolf. Wants me there tomorrow after breakfast.' He stared at his parents and shrugged. 'And we're to tell no one. No one!'

Thirty-six

'They'll be all right? Won't they?' Amy asked as they watched Ed and Jessica cycle off down the road.

Rick smiled at her. 'Of course! They're sensible kids.' He looked at her more closely. 'What's worrying you?'

Amy shook her head. 'You don't think,' she said slowly, 'that one of those ranchers might knock them over, or something?'

Rick put his arm round her shoulders. 'Hey!' he reproached. 'You're getting paranoid. They'll be fine. It's only a kilometre. They'll be back in an hour.'

Jimmy Skagawa met them in the road halfway there. He looked serious. 'My grandpa's waiting for you.

I'm bringing you to him.' They pedalled in silence to the huddle of motor trailers and single-storey shacks where Jimmy's large family lived.

Dogs ran barking to meet them. A few hens scratched in the dirt. A woman was hanging out washing on a sagging line between two trees. There was no one else about. Jessica thought she saw a curtain move.

They went up the steps of the biggest motor home. Someone was growing tomatoes beside the door. 'Go on in,' Jimmy told them. Ed hesitated in the doorway.

'No need to be shy!' called an old, cracked voice. They went inside. Facing them in a small armchair was the oldest person they had ever seen. His face was seamed with a thousand fine lines. His hair was pure white and hung in a thick plait across his shoulders. His hands were small and brown and twisted with arthritis. They lay claw-like in his lap. But his eyes were humorous and kind.

He smiled at them. 'Jimmy tells me you're the boy who let the wolf go free.'

Ed nodded.

The old man studied him. 'That was good,' he said at last. 'And brave.' He looked at Jessica. 'There used to be many wolves around here when I was young. They only killed what was sick or old. We lived in peace with them then, before the ranchers came.' He paused. 'I hear your wolf is back.'

'They were howling last night,' Jessica told him shyly. 'Out near the Daniels' ranch.'

'Excuse me!' Ed interrupted. 'Did you say *MY* wolf?'

The question seemed to please the old man. He smiled and gave a nod of approval. 'Jimmy told me you were smart.' He stared up at the boy. 'Two days ago,' he explained, 'one of my sons, Joseph, saw him crossing the road ten miles north of here. A big, black wolf. The biggest wolf he ever saw. He had a female with him.'

Ed's face broke into a huge grin. It was the confirmation he had been waiting for. 'That's my wolf!' he cried. 'That's him!'

'He's come back,' the old man agreed. 'So he's smart too!' and he chuckled. It sounded like sand in a biscuit tin. 'This is good country for a wolf.'

'They're going to kill him!' Jessica told him. 'Daniels and the other ranchers. They've got a helicopter as well!'

'But if we can find him first,' Ed burst out, 'my

dad will tranquillize him. And his mate. Then we can get 'em taken to the Yellowstone National Park.'

'Where they'll be safe!' added Jessica. 'For ever!'

'Can you help us?' Ed pleaded. 'Do you know where we could find him?'

'There's only the four of us,' Jessica told the old man.

'And hundreds of others who want him dead,' Ed added.

'The sheriff's one of them!' Jessica exclaimed. 'I don't like him. He's a creep.' The old man beckoned them closer.

'My name is Little Wolf,' he told them. 'It was my father's name and his father's before that. My family understand the wolf. Now I will talk with my sons. Maybe they can find out where the wolf is sleeping.'

Ed looked at Jessica and grinned.

Little Wolf sat up in his chair. Jessica saw that his hands were shaking. They looked so frail. She beamed at him. 'Thank you very much!' she said. It sounded such a dull thing to say.

Little Wolf cleared his throat. 'If we find the wolf,' he continued, 'my son Joseph will call your father. He must do whatever Joseph tells him.' He frowned and hesitated, picking his words carefully. 'One more thing,' he told them. 'You must stay away from here! Never come back! Tell no one you have been. You must promise this.'

His voice trembled and Jessica was startled by its intensity. His chest rose and fell. 'Men with power, like the ranchers or the sheriff, can make life very hard for people like us. For our sakes, be careful, and be patient!'

Thirty-seven

The call came through six days later, just after supper. A tentative voice said, 'This is Joseph. Is that Rick?' And went on, 'I think we've found your friend. Can we meet up early tomorrow? At the old timber mill by the river? You can park out of sight round the back. Bring a good map.'

Rick replaced the phone and beamed round at his family. The next moment they were all whooping with joy, hugging each other in relief, the strain of the past week now allowed to show.

'I'll be there bright and early,' Rick told them.

'Wrong!' Amy laughed, wagging a finger under his nose. 'We'll *all* be there at the crack of dawn!'

The next morning, there was still a heavy dew on the grass when Rick left the road and drove cautiously down an overgrown track. There were old wooden buildings on either side with weeds growing out of the windows. Jessica had a brief glimpse of a huge rusty saw and piles of grey sawdust. Then they were turning into a small yard and nosing towards a battered red car.

'That must be him!' cried Amy, pointing as a man came out of a broken doorway and waved to them. He was tall, with glossy, black hair. He was wearing a khaki shirt and a faded pair of jeans. And for some reason, Ed liked him at once.

'I'm your man!' he told them. 'The name's Joseph.' And they all shook hands. He had a large silver wolf's head on his belt buckle. He gripped Ed by the shoulders and looked at him for a moment. 'You've been a good friend to little Jimmy,' he said, with a smile. 'Now you're my friend too!' Ed grinned back.

'Well,' he said, looking round at their expectant faces. 'Let me tell you what's been happening. We've found your wolf and – Wow! – he's a big boy!'

'Black all over?' Ed asked, aware of his heart racing. Jimmy's grandfather had told him it was the same wolf. His wolf. But he had to be certain. For some reason, Nature was putting them together again.

Joseph nodded. 'Pure black. All over.'

Rick was unfolding a map and laying it on the bonnet of the pick-up. Amy smiled warmly at Joseph. 'You're brilliant!' she said. 'How on earth did you find him?'

Joseph put a large finger against the side of his nose and winked. 'Lady,' he told her, 'my people have lived round here a long time. We can still think like a wolf when we have to!'

He peered at the map. 'Your wolf's holed up in the woods above Lost Boy Canyon. Just about here!' He jabbed at the map. Ed looked at the swirl of contour lines, not sure what to think.

'He's got a female with him,' Joseph went on. 'His mate. She's in cub. It's starting to show.'

Rick nodded. 'How close can we get?'

Joseph thought for a moment. 'Depends how much noise you make.' Then he chuckled. 'Those wolves live pretty well. Plenty of deer. Most of the time, they're sleeping out in the sun. There's a pile of rocks a hundred metres away. Upwind, usually.' He looked at Rick quizzically. 'You aiming to tranquillize them?'

Rick rubbed his jaw. 'It'll have to be a neck or shoulders shot. It won't be easy.'

Joseph shrugged. 'I can maybe get in closer if you like.'

'How do we get out there?' Amy wanted to know. 'It's right in the middle of nowhere.'

The man smiled at her. 'See here!' He traced his thumbnail across the map. 'We're lucky! There's an old logging road running up the canyon. It's passable. The ranch people use it occasionally.'

'Which ranch people?' asked Ed. 'Whose land is it?'

'Your friend Daniels',' Joseph told him, 'but they only go there at round-up time.' He turned back to Rick. 'It's a long, steep walk from the canyon,' he warned. 'You've got to be silent all the way.'

'I can do it,' protested Jessica. 'I'm much quieter than Ed.'

Rick looked at Amy and nodded. 'You just say when, Joseph!' He put a hand on the man's arm. 'Then I'll contact the Yellowstone folks.'

Joseph grinned. 'I'll be back out tomorrow. They're due a kill. So be ready. I'll meet you on the track. They won't hear us down there.' He pulled a piece of paper out of his pocket. 'Give me your mobile number.'

'Great!' Rick exclaimed. 'Let's go for it!'

The Viccarys piled back inside their pick-up and drove away, waving frantically.

'Careful!' Amy snapped a few moments later as they reached the road. 'Something coming!' They waited until the 4 x 4 went speeding past on the other side, then pulled out.

Half a mile down the road, Mel gave an exclamation and braked to a long, sliding halt. That had been the Viccarys' truck. Those New York plates were unmistakable.

What the heck were they doing at the old mill? He wrenched the wheel round in a tight turn and roared back in a cloud of dust. A car was just leaving the place. An old red Cadillac that had seen better days. Mel recognized it at once. And the driver.

He picked a dead match out of the ashtray and began chewing on it. Why would the Viccarys be talking to Joseph Skagawa? The only thing he was any good for was finding lost cattle during the October round-up. And he was brilliant at that. Fifty metres further on, he swerved violently, almost clipping a telegraph pole.

Mel drove at top speed back to the ranch. He burst into the office and found the rancher deep in conversation with Sheriff Hoskins. They stared at him. 'Looks like you won the jackpot,' the sheriff said easily.

'What's up?' Daniels demanded.

Mel told them. Daniels' chair went over with a crash. His face flamed. 'No flies on Viccary!' he shouted angrily. 'That guy's too damn smart!' He swung round on the sheriff. 'Skagawa's the best tracker in the state. I know! I've seen what he can do. He knows every rock, every stream, for miles!'

He drummed his fingers. 'There's only one reason he'd be meeting Viccary! He's gonna find this wolf for him! Damn it! They've got the jump on us! Now what do we do?' He glared furiously at the impassive bulk of the sheriff.

Sheriff Hoskins said nothing. Instead, he unfolded a fresh stick of chewing gum and slid it carefully into his mouth. He chewed a couple of times then beamed at them. He uttered one word. 'Technology!'

They stared at him uncomprehendingly. 'What the heck's that supposed to mean?' the rancher demanded.

The sheriff looked as if he was enjoying himself. He repeated the word and added, 'We've got one of those satellite tracking things back at HQ. Neat little piece. Accurate to within three metres, I'm told. Never had reason to use it, so far.'

Their eyes grew wider, as he continued, 'Perhaps we should give it a little test. I'll stop by the Viccary place later on tonight. It won't take two shakes of a dog's tail to place it under their vehicle!'

Daniels shook his head in admiration and clapped him on the shoulder. 'I don't know what we'd do without you, Steve!' he said admiringly.

The sheriff looked modest. 'Hey! That's my job! Like the badge says. I'm just here to serve and protect!'

Thirty-eight

Marak had an itch. An itch that wouldn't go away. Right between his shoulder blades. He didn't want to move. The sun was hot. He had eaten too much and now he was feeling drowsy. His eyelids stayed closed.

Beside him, Ootak gave a sigh and got carefully to her feet. The cubs were moving inside her and she couldn't get comfortable. She stood over him and yawned. Then bent and licked his nose.

She turned away and walked slowly to the hide they had made under the roots of the old fir tree. It was cool in there. She snapped at the swarm of flies that hung round her head, then squeezed inside.

Marak could bear it no longer. He swung over on his back and for a moment lay like a puppy with his legs in the air. Then he began to wriggle around in a luxurious scratch. He collapsed on his side and sank into a dreamless sleep. Occasionally, he flapped an ear when the flies became too aggressive. Otherwise there was only the hum of insects and the smell of warm earth to pay attention to.

A hundred metres away, Rick stared at him through telescopic sights. He could count individual bristles along the wolf's jaws. He stared fascinated at the rhythmic rise and fall of the animal's sides.

Joseph nudged him and raised a thumb in query. It was time. Rick pulled the rifle butt hard into his shoulder. It would need two darts to tranquillize a wolf this size. He would have to reload fast. He peered through the sights.

There was a loud, angry buzzing in his ear. He looked around and almost dropped the rifle in fright. A hornet the size of his thumb had landed on top of the sight, a couple of centimetres from his face. His head whirled in panic, suddenly full of childhood warnings. 'Five hornet stings to kill a horse. One for a human!'

He stared in horror at the bright yellow body with its red warning bands. The hornet was moving across the wooden rifle stock towards his fingers. His eyes shut tight. He could feel its feet moving across his skin. It stopped moving and he guessed it was drinking his sweat.

It seemed to last an eternity before he realized it had flown off. He opened his eyes and found Joseph lying rigid beside him. They stared at each other and saw the relief in the other's face.

Meanwhile, Marak was getting bored being on his own. The two men watched him sit up, yawn and disappear into the dark shadow under the tree. There was nothing they could do. Only wait.

Time was also hanging heavy for Amy and the others waiting by the pick-up. Rick had parked it, at Joseph's suggestion, facing the way they had come. There were two full-length stretchers in the back. Joseph's car was close by.

There was not a breath of air in the canyon and very little shade. Just bare rocks spilling over on to the track. Sweat was soon running down all their faces.

'Why can't we wait up there, under the trees,' Jessica pointed. 'It's too hot. It's scorching!'

'She's right, Mum!' Ed insisted. 'We can't stay here. We'll get heat exhaustion!'

Amy hesitated. 'I guess you're right,' she agreed.

'But we've got to keep the vehicles in sight. So we can see your father and Joseph coming back.'

'That could be hours,' complained Jessica.

'Well, you wanted to come!' Amy reminded her tartly.

They climbed up the rock-strewn hillside towards the line of trees and were out of breath by the time they reached them. But it was worth it. It was deliciously cool there. They each had a drink of water, then sat down and waited. Time passed. Amy took out a book. Jessica began to make patterns with pine cones. Both were engrossed, when Ed said suddenly, 'There's a car coming!' He scrambled to his feet.

'Ed!' Amy called. 'Wait!' And then, 'Come back!'

A sudden fear gripped the boy. He ran out into the sunshine, picking his way down through the rocks. The track was hidden by a screen of overhanging bushes, but he could hear the car quite clearly. Whoever these people were, he thought, they were driving far too fast. Almost as if they had a particular reason for coming here.

A cloud of dust swirled towards him. He caught a flash of yellow as the car braked. He stared in horror. A police car! And a truck close behind. The dust billowed up to engulf him. He heard doors slamming and men's voices. It was not true! This was not happening! It couldn't be!

Thirty-nine

Marak woke with a growl in his throat. He lay perfectly still in the darkness, wide awake. Concentrating. Something had woken him. An unfamiliar sound. He tested the air, but could find nothing unusual.

Ootak was still asleep. He looked at her and his tail began to wag. He looked away, hurriedly. He must not let Ootak distract him. Something had brought him out of a deep sleep. He stole forward to the entrance and listened. Nothing. And yet, he felt danger growing around them.

A low snarl brought Ootak to his side. He stepped outside into the sunlight, narrowing his eyes against the glare, and looked around. Nothing. He stared at the rocks and into the shadows between them.

Something was moving in there! A flicker of black in the gloom. He barked a warning and heard a crack like a branch breaking. A sharp, stinging blow hit him on the shoulder. Furiously, he bit at the yellow wasp-like creature. The pain was intense. It radiated from the dart.

Marak chased round and round, snarling loudly, trying to free himself of it. Another crack, and the same piercing sensation. He glared at the rocks and at the bushes that covered them. A branch was quivering. He barked at it and turned to run after Ootak.

But something was wrong. His body felt detached. Everything seemed to be happening so slowly. His legs were curiously stiff. They wouldn't bend. There was no feeling in his shoulder. His feet were skidding over the ground. The great muscles in his back legs almost powerless. His mouth was dry. He staggered. The sky was lurching above his head.

He could hear voices. Men's voices! In front of him. Closing in. Getting nearer. Too near. Run! He blinked helplessly and peered around. A boy was racing towards him. He could see the way his legs were lifting up and down. And the exhaustion on the boy's face. His mouth was wide open.

Marak shook his head, trying to clear the growing fog. The boy's scent was strong. Familiar! The cage! Marak backed away. Confused. There was another human behind the boy. Pushing him out of the way. Pounding towards the wolf. Marak tried to turn and leave them all behind.

His head was spinning. He slipped down on to one knee. When he looked up, the big man was almost on top of him. His arms were swinging down towards Marak. They were holding a long stick.

The wolf looked directly into the man's eyes as the first shot exploded. For a millisecond, Marak remembered the red helicopter and the boy tugging open the cage door. He was dead before the sheriff fired the second time.

Ootak heard the shots and guessed their meaning. But she did not slacken her pace. Marak's cubs were alive inside her. They were all that mattered now. Nature would not allow her to make a pointless sacrifice. She must get as far away as possible from this place of death. She would mourn Marak later.

The crack of the gunshots faded into the brightness of the afternoon. A terrible silence fell, only broken by the sobbing of the boy. Slowly, dazedly, Rick stood up and walked unsteadily towards his son.

Behind him, Joseph screamed abuse. The sheriff's rifle swung towards him. 'Make my day!' he warned. Other men appeared. Mel and a uniformed patrolman. Mel gave a shout and slapped his sides in triumph. Ed was on his feet, his fists swinging. Sheriff Hoskins grabbed him and pulled him back.

'OK, boy!' he said calmly. 'Nothing you can do about it now!' Then to Mel, 'You just stay right there,' he shouted. 'Don't come any closer. That's an order!'

Rick led his son away and hugged him very tightly. Too shocked to say anything. The wolf lay stretched full-length on the ground. He seemed to be smiling. The patrolman produced a camera and took photographs. The buzz of flies grew thicker. The sheriff shuffled his feet, then slowly walked away. He touched his hat to Amy and Jessica as they appeared, hot and anxious. Mel followed him and never looked back.

The Viccarys gathered round the wolf, not knowing what to say or do. Conscious only of the terrible waste of it all. Marak's eyes were beginning to glaze. At some stage, Joseph went back to the vehicles and returned, carrying two spades and an army blanket. Everyone took their turn digging. When it was deep enough, they wrapped Marak in the blanket and gently lowered him in.

Ed stood looking down into the grave, knowing that Nature, for a brief moment, had let him get very close. That he had played a part in all this tragedy. He no longer cried. Anger had seared his tears for the moment. Instead, a fierce determination was growing inside him. He would spend the rest of his life fighting to stop the slaughter. To end the terrible waste.

He took the spade from Joseph and drove it into the pile of earth. He held it out over the grave and let the spoil fall gently across the wolf's body. When it was finished and the grave filled in, Ed looked over at his mother's tear-stained face. He went to her and they stood for a long time, silently holding one another.

Later, Rick put his arms around both his children's shoulders and led them away. Jessica's crying faded into the afternoon and the sounds of the forest cautiously returned. At sunset, a little breeze sighed and blew sand over the stains on the ground.

Later that night, the moon appeared and bathed the ground in brilliant light. A mouse scurried into the open. It saw the gleam of an empty cartridge case and stood upright in alarm. Its nose twitched busily, catching the acrid smell. Then it sneezed and turned away, disappearing into a little tunnel in the grass. From the top of a tree, a white owl tilted its head and marked the spot for the future.

In Little Wolf's motor trailer, the old man held Ed and Jessica's hands. He looked at them with his steady brown eyes, knowing the hurt and the anger they were suffering. Eventually he spoke. 'The wolf is dead. Yes! But remember, he will live on through his cubs . . . We all do . . .'

Postscript

Ootak had six cubs. Two of them pure black like their father. Of the other cubs, one was shot by a hunter. Another was run over by a logging truck. The rest are still alive and living somewhere in the forests of the western Rockies.

Rick and Amy left Elliott Lake soon after Marak's death and went to work for the Yellowstone National Park's Wolf Resettlement Project. The family are all very happy there. Ed wants to go to college in due course and study zoology. After that, he wants to work with animals in the wild. Right now, he's not sure where.

Jessica has not made up her mind what she wants to do but thinks she'll become a vet. Her parents believe she'll make a very good one.

Pete Daniels was recently voted 'The Boy Most Likely to Succeed', at his school. He has – almost – forgotten Ed Viccary.

Little Wolf is dead. Joseph scattered his ashes over Marak's grave. Joseph often goes back to sit on the ground in the sunshine and to listen to what the wolves are thinking.

It is now illegal to shoot wolves anywhere in the USA.

Also by Geoffrey Malone, from Hodder Children's Books

KIMBA

Kimba was born among the boulders of M'Goma Hill, in the scorching heat of the afternoon.

Nurtured by his mother, fierce, tender Sabba, he learns the ways of the plains: the merciless hunt for food, the dangers from ravenous hyenas, leopards, snakes, crocodiles – and rival lions.

But when strange lions challenge his father, Blank Mane, for leadership of the pride, Kimba is running for his life . . .

Now he must hunt alone. Somehow he must grow fiercer, more powerful, more formidable . . . Ready to challenge for leadership of his old pride, ready to face lion's greatest enemy . . . Man.

Also by Geoffrey Malone, from Hodder Children's Books

TORN EAR

The wind carried the scent of blood far into the night, while the vixen still pawed at the broken little bodies on the pile of earth.

But Torn Ear survives the gamekeeper's attack. Slowly his mother introduces him to the fox's world – the skills of hunting and how to avoid danger.

Then he is on his own.

Until he meets Velvet, and they have their own cubs. But man intervenes again, and his favourite cub is threatened. Torn Ear must rescue her, but will he escape the clutches of the gamekeeper this time?

ELEPHANT BEN

Ben is travelling in the African Plains with his game-ranger father. It's a chance he's longed for, to really see the animals in the wild.

This territory is roamed by the great elephant Temba and her family in their daily hunt for food, their battles against ravenous lions and crocodiles who prey on young elephant calves.

But, unknown to Ben, other humans are near. And their interest in the elephants is very different. For Temba and her family – and for Ben – a terrifying battle for survival awaits . . .